The Midnight Watchers Christmas

NELL HARTE

VIDORRA HOUSE

©Copyright 2023 Nell Harte

All Rights Reserved

License Notes

This Book is licensed for personal enjoyment only. It may not be resold. No part of this work may be reproduced in any form or by any electronic or mechanical means including information storage and retrieval systems, without written permission from the author.

Disclaimer

This story is a work of fiction, any resemblance to people is purely coincidence. All places, names, events, businesses, etc. are used in a fictional manner. All characters are from the imagination of the author.

Table of Contents

Chapter One *1*

Chapter Two *11*

Chapter Three *23*

Chapter Four *33*

Chapter Five *43*

Chapter Six *51*

Chapter Seven *59*

Chapter Eight *67*

Chapter Nine *77*

Chapter Ten *85*

Chapter Eleven *95*

Chapter Twelve *101*

Chapter Thirteen *107*

Chapter Fourteen *125*

Chapter Fifteen *137*

Chapter Sixteen *143*

Chapter Seventeen *151*

Chapter Eighteen *161*

Chapter Nineteen *171*

Chapter Twenty 181

Chapter Twenty-One 189

Chapter Twenty-Two..................................... 195

Epilogue.. 201

PREVIEW... 210

  The Blind Tailor's Daughter 211

  Chapter One 213

  Chapter Two 223

Chapter One

Edinburgh, 1856

Snow lay thick on the ground, blanketing the cobblestones. Fat flakes floated down from heavy laden skies, kissing the nipped cheeks of those hurrying home to warm fireplaces and warmer families. Giddy students from the university hurled snowballs at one another, oblivious to the cold, for they wore coats of potent brandy and merriment, their hearts full of the promise of Christmas. And across the city, bells chimed ten o'clock, while sweet voices rose up to the heavens from St. Giles' Cathedral, practicing hymns for the Christmas evensong.

It was Fiona McVey's favourite day—not Christmas itself, not Christmas Eve either, but the night of the 21st. Her father liked to say they were keeping with old traditions, celebrating Yule the way their ancestors might have, but Fiona had always suspected there was more to it, for her mother and father never missed a Sunday at church and her mother prayed every night by the bed. Not exactly the actions of a pagan.

"He's late," Fiona said, drumming her fingertips against the worn surface of the kitchen table.

Her mother, Beryl, chuckled brightly. "You shouldn't be starting the celebrations in a foul mood, Fiona." She had an Edinburgh lilt, a far cry from her husband's broad brogue. "He'll be up when he's up. Mr. Walker will be having him working his fingers to the bone, right up 'til Christmas Eve. You know what it's like at this time of year."

"I know." Fiona puffed out a breath, her twelve-year-old heart eager to begin the celebrations… and to devour the huge feast that her mother had spent the past two days cooking.

It had all been laid out on the kitchen table: little cheese and onion tarts, boiled, sweet langoustines fresh from the sea, a dressed crab, an entire ham studded with cloves, and flaky salmon that would melt in the mouth. Places had been reserved for the hot dishes that were keeping warm in the wood stove: the crispy potatoes, honeyed carrots, and the crown of the feast—the roast goose. Even hidden from view, the smell was a torment, making Fiona's mouth water.

"Can I have just one mince pie?" she pleaded, eyeing up the puddings at the farthest end of the table: a figgy pudding that would flicker with blue flames when her father soaked it in brandy and lit it; a whole plate of sugar dusted mince pies; a pyramid of spiced apple puffs, and currant dotted Bannocks, among so many more. They would be eating it all for days, and nothing would make Fiona happier.

Beryl plucked up a mince pie and handed it to her eager daughter. "Just the one, but if you don't eat your roast goose, I'll not be pleased."

"I haven't eaten all day to prepare!" Fiona took the delicacy gratefully, saying a silent word of gratitude before biting down. The taste of dried fruit and spices and butter and sugar melted on her tongue, her soul singing along with the choir in the distance.

Beryl untied her apron and hung it by the kitchen door. "Is it nice?"

"Heaven, Mama," Fiona replied with her mouth full, crumbs tumbling. "I could take one up the street to Pa. Might encourage him to come home quicker."

"You stay where you are. He'll be done soon enough," Beryl insisted, sitting opposite.

Fiona's father, Donal McVey, was the finest clockmaker in all of Scotland, employed by a wealthy man by the name of Mr. Walker at a prestigious shop in the New Town, aptly—or rather unaptly—named *Walker's Clocks and Clockworks.* Mr. Walker himself, on the other hand, would not know what to do with a cog or a dial if his life depended upon it. That was what Fiona's father said when he was at home, knowing he could not be overheard, but the work paid well and allowed the McVeys a comfortable existence in their cosy New Town apartments, overlooking the greenery of Princes Street Gardens.

"Eat your mince pie and be grateful," Beryl said, not unkindly, as she dabbed the sweat of the kitchen from her brow. "We'll have our merriment soon enough."

Fiona relented. "Why is he so busy at Christmas? You'd think he'd be less busy, since the shop is shut for two whole days!"

"He's just... a very dedicated man," Beryl replied with a secret smile.

As if summoned, the rattle of keys jingled through the apartments, followed by the strained squeal of unoiled hinges. Fiona sat bolt upright, her heart leaping as she listened to the familiar symphony of her father stamping his boots on the mat, scraping off the outside world, and the thudding rock of the coat stand as he hung up his coat. Softer footfalls crossed the entrance hall, and then, to Fiona's delight, the kitchen door swung open and her father poked his head around.

"I heard there was some sort of hootenanny here tonight," Donal said, grinning. "I dinnae have me an invitation, but I'm hopin' ye'll take pity on a lad with a growlin' stomach."

"Papa!" Fiona jumped up and flew at him, throwing her arms around his waist and hugging him tight.

Donal hugged her back, pressing a kiss to her wild, dark hair that desperately needed a brushing. "Sorry I'm late, me wee ducklin'."

"You're not late," she hugged him tighter, "you're just in time. I had a mince pie."

"Ye did? Eeh, ye wee imp!" He chuckled. "Ye'd better eat all yer goose, else yer ma willnae ever make us a feast like this again."

Fiona peered up at her father's face, pinched red by the cold. "I told mama already; I've been preparing for this all day. Haven't eaten a thing."

"Ye're a wise one, lass," Donal said, pressing another kiss to her brow, before he made his way to his wife, who stood waiting with her arms wide open.

Fiona pulled a face, turning her gaze away as her father swept her mother into a fond embrace, bending his head to kiss her deeply as if they had only married yesterday instead of five-and-ten years ago. Beryl melted into her husband's affection, the two of them dancing slowly around the kitchen for a moment or two, their lips never leaving one another's. It was the same every night and every morning, and though Fiona knew she ought to feel lucky that her parents loved one another so much, and so openly, she wished they would not show it in front of her quite so often.

"Can we eat now?" she said grumpily. "I've been waiting *forever*!"

The besotted pair parted, save for their clasped hands, casting adoring smiles at one another as they took their places at the table, prompting Fiona to slide back into her usual chair.

"It looks wonderful," Donal said, leaning over to kiss his wife's rosy cheek. "The feast doesnae look too shabby either."

Beryl batted him playfully away. "Fiona will kill us if we don't start eating soon." She shot up. "I'd forgotten the goose! You're a mischief, Donal McVey—all that kissing, and I'd forget my own head if it wasn't attached to my neck."

"I cannae help meself." Donal grinned, reaching across the table for a bottle of red wine that a client of the clockmakers had given him as a gift for fixing a very old grandfather clock that everyone else had said was beyond repair.

As Beryl fetched the warm dishes, placing them reverently into the empty spots on the feasting table, Donal poured two hearty glasses for him and his wife, while fresh-pressed apple juice was Fiona's chosen tipple. She did not like the taste of wine, and though her parents said she would when she was older, she doubted it.

"Hands together," Beryl insisted, the trio joining hands, though it meant Fiona awkwardly raising her elbow above the glistening ham. "Say your prayers, and once you're done, we can begin."

It was the same every time they dined, even if it was just a simple breakfast, the three of them closing their eyes and silently saying whatever was in their hearts, keeping their prayers to themselves. Sometimes, Fiona cheated and did not say a prayer at all, but that night, she *did* have something to say.

Thank you for everything we have. Thank you for giving us good fortune from my father's hard work. Thank you for honouring us with your kindness, she thought as loudly as she could, hoping, that way, it might reach the heavens. *Thank you for this glorious feast, and I hope there are many others tonight, and in the days to come, enjoying warmth and joy like this. To those who can't, I hope there will be happiness for them soon, and I hope that, one day, I will have enough to share to everyone I meet.*

They were the hopes of a naïve girl, but she meant them keenly, even if she did not know how she might make that happen. At her age, with no dream insurmountable, anything was possible as long as she believed it was.

"Are we all done?" Beryl asked.

Fiona opened her eyes and nodded effusively. "I wished for everyone to be this lucky. I wished that everyone could be happy this Christmas. And I wished that, one day, when I'm older, I might be able to make lots and lots of people as happy as I am now."

A strange look passed between Beryl and Donal, their sparkling eyes speaking a secret language that Fiona did not always understand. She ignored it and jabbed a slice of ham with her fork, flopping it down onto her plate.

"Thank you, Mama," she said, about to take her first delicious bite of the salty sweet ham that had been brined and baked and glazed to perfection.

She had just popped the morsel into her mouth when her father said, "Fiona, there's somethin' we should tell ye. Somethin' we've nae told ye because we were nae certain ye were ready." He paused. "I think ye're ready now."

"What is it?" Fiona chewed contentedly, washing the ham down with some apple juice.

Donal glanced at Beryl again, who nodded her encouragement. "I think it's time ye learned what it is I do on Christmas Eve and Christmas Day—why we celebrate tonight instead of then. And why I... work so late in the weeks before Christmas."

"Because Mr. Walker is a crank," Fiona said.

Donal erupted into laughter, while Beryl pretended to disapprove, smiling all the while, as she served her husband and daughter with thick, juicy slices of roast goose and golden potatoes.

Fiona's eyes widened. "What? That's what you always say."

"It's naught to do with Mr. Walker, for though he *is* a crank, he's more generous than most when it gets to Christmas," Donal explained, dabbing at his amused, teary eyes. "Truth be told, I wouldnae be able to do what it is I do if Mr. Walker had me workin' like the lads at the factories or the fellas at the mills."

Fiona cut into her goose, inhaling the tantalising smells. "What is it you do? You don't go drinking like those noisy students, do you?"

"I daenae," her father replied, grinning. "I… make toys, and I give 'em out to those who need 'em the most."

Fiona paused, a forkful of goose halfway to her mouth. "Pardon?"

"All through the year, I spend a few hours in me workshop after I'm done at Mr. Walker's, makin' toys. Wooden toys, mostly, but if I can find enough clockwork pieces that nay one is usin', I'll make some clockwork toys too. Mr. Walker doesn't miss the parts he doesnae need, and he wouldnae ken what he needed even so. But I *do* buy some of me own parts when I can," her father said, between mouthfuls of his own goose and potatoes. "Late on Christmas Eve and all through Christmas Day mornin', I put 'em all into sacks and I take 'em through the Old Town, handin' 'em out for the bairns who might nae have anythin' to look forward to."

Fiona stared at him in disbelief, so shocked she had to set down her fork and knife. "You do that every year?"

"This'll be me seventh year," he told her with a nod. "And if ye're willin', I wondered if ye might help me this year. We can always use extra hands."

Fiona looked to her mother. "Do you help, too? I've never seen you sneak out."

"I stay with you," Beryl replied, taking hold of her husband's hand. "But I am always proud of my darling and his tireless work. His toys are beautiful. Absolutely beautiful. Better than anything you can find in the toyshops."

Donal blushed. "Och, I do me best with what I have."

"And you want *me* to come and help?" A shiver of excitement ran through Fiona, tinged with an undercurrent of fear, for the Old Town was a dark place across the divide of Princes Street Gardens. A place she would never have dared to tread alone, for all of her friends at school told stories of that sprawling slum, filling her mind with terrifying tales of robbery and murder and worse.

But if pa goes there every year, and he's not afraid, why should I be? she told herself, bolstering her courage. Indeed, how bad could it be? She knew nothing of poverty, not really, and had always assumed that the stories of her school friends were deliberately farfetched. She could already imagine the stories that *she* would tell her friends, when she discovered that they were sorely mistaken, and that she had gone there with her father, completely unafraid. They would think her the bravest girl in Edinburgh.

"If ye'd like to," her father urged. "Ye said ye wanted people to be happy, and when they see them toys, ducklin', they *are* happy. There's nae sight more pleasin', I promise ye."

Chewing heartily on a carefully constructed mouthful of goose, redcurrant jam, crispy potato, honeyed carrot, and a little bit of ham, Fiona nodded with all the mettle of a twelve-year-old who had no idea what she would face in that shadowed realm beyond the pleasant park. "I'll do it!" she cheered, raising her glass of apple juice. "Merry Christmas to all, and to all a Merry Christmas!"

"Merry Christmas!" her mother and father responded, clinking her glass with theirs.

And as they ate and drank and truly were merry, while snow fell beyond the frosty windows and the bells continued to chime, Fiona's fears faded to nothing. For at a time like this, when all was right and beautiful with the world, how could there possibly be any darkness within it?

Chapter Two

Christmas Eve arrived with a fresh fall of snow, turning the air crisp and fresh, the city muffled to a peaceful silence. Fiona and her mother had enjoyed a fine day together, purchasing the last few things for Boxing Day, when they would share another, smaller celebration. Fiona had never understood why they treated Boxing Day as if it were Christmas Day, but now she did; it was a celebration to reward her father's efforts, to give him the rest he had missed out on while helping others.

"Put on yer thickest coat," her father said, throwing a satchel over his shoulder. "It's bitter out there, and ye'll be out in it 'til dawn."

Fiona reached for the ermine trimmed coat that her mother had bought her the previous year, but her father shook his head. "Not that'un. The one without the fur on it. Ye can put on one of me scarves to keep yer neck warm."

"But my ermine is the warmest," Fiona tried to protest.

"The other one," Donal insisted.

Fiona did not understand why she could not wear her very best, very warmest coat, but she was too anxious and excited to argue any further. Taking down her simpler, black coat, she buttoned it quickly, her hands trembling slightly. The coat swept the floor, covering up the woollen, light pink day dress she wore beneath.

"I packed sandwiches for the two of you," Beryl said, appearing in the entrance hall, looking as nervous as Fiona felt. "Some of the leftover ham and a swipe of piccalilli." She passed a waxed paper parcel to Donal, who slipped it into his satchel and leaned over to kiss his wife.

"Thank ye, love." He winked and took down a bright red scarf, wrapping it around Fiona's face and neck, until only her eyes peeked out. She laughed into the wool, the steam of her breath dampening her concealed face.

Beryl pulled her daughter and husband to her. "Be safe, won't you?"

"I wouldnae let aught happen to either of us," Donal promised, squeezing back. "We'll be home in time for breakfast, love. Daenae fret."

With nothing more to say and a night's worth of gift-giving to begin, father and daughter headed out of the apartments, while Beryl stood in the doorway and waved as they made their way down the staircase to the main entrance. Fiona waved back as if she were on her way to a carnival, grinning from ear to ear, while Donal opened the door. A blast of icy wind pinched the back of Fiona's head, dulling her enthusiasm for a moment.

"Ye'll warm up soon enough," her father told her, as if reading her mind. "Come on, we've nae a moment to lose."

He offered Fiona his hand and she took it gratefully with her gloved one, letting him lead her through the dark evening towards East Princes Street Gardens.

At the black iron gate that opened into the park, Fiona stopped and looked ahead, wondering if this was what it was like for sailors aboard a ship, seeing foreign and fearsome lands for the first time.

The Old Town was a different country entirely, crammed with people she did not know, people who did not come to the New Town, people who kept to their landlocked island of ill-repute for the same reason no one from the New Town ventured across—they came from two opposite worlds, and neither was interested in the other.

"Is it safe?" Fiona whispered, suddenly wishing she was back in the heat of the apartments, curled up with her mother whilst they read books and ate Bannocks with sugary cups of tea.

Donal gave his daughter's hand a squeeze. "I wouldnae take ye if it wasnae." He paused. "But if ye tire or ye get too cold or ye decide ye daenae want to continue, I can take ye home whenever ye please. All ye need do is ask."

"I'll... do my best," Fiona promised, taking a breath as she passed through the gate, snowflakes kissing her cheeks and prompting her to bury the lower half of her face deeper into the scarf.

She clung to her father's hand as he guided her through the snow and shadows, both keeping their heads down as they walked by inebriates and beggars who seemed to be asleep on the benches, oblivious to the icy weather, some of them covered in a snowy blanket all their own.

Some were just lumps of white, while others barked unintelligibly at Fiona and her father, waving a jar of something. Likely the 'Mother's Ruin' that the girls at her school were always whispering about.

The pair cut straight across the gardens and up a harsh slope on the other side, emerging onto a cobbled street. The streetlamps had been lit, casting a fuzzy glow across the dirty snow, trampled underfoot by countless boots and shoes, yet Fiona could not see a single person.

The streets were empty; eerily so, as if everyone had simply vanished. Even at night in the New Town, no matter the weather, there were always *some* people wandering around.

Walking parallel to the gardens, they turned left up a steep, curved street. Fiona gripped her father's hand tighter, terrified she might slip on the slick cobbles and end up sliding right down to the bottom.

Almost in sight of what she knew to be the Royal Mile, her father pulled her sharply through a pitch-black passageway. Panicked, she tried not to lose her balance, unable to see her father though he could not have been more than a foot's length in front of her, and her hand was still in his.

"Here," he said, stopping beside a doorway cut into the wall. A quiet jangle of keys followed in the thick darkness, then the soft hiss of a door opening. "Mind yer head," he said, tugging her hand gently. The lintel was low, and he had to duck to get inside whatever lay beyond, but she could pass through without having to bend at all.

He left her in the gloom, his hand letting go of hers before she could utter a word of protest.

But then lanterns began to fade into life, casting strange shapes onto patchy walls, bringing the room where she stood into view, piece by piece.

It was a workshop, with a long, weathered workbench in the centre, strewn with corrugated snakes of shaved wood, splashes of colourful paint, jars filled with brushes, and a neat array of tools laid out on a length of old cloth.

And the walls were heavy with shelves and crooked bookcases, every available bit of space laden down with toys. Toys of all kinds: woollen-haired dolls, nutcrackers in full regalia, horses set upon wheels with a string to pull them along, spinning tops in rainbow colours, detailed little frogs with ridged backs, among thousands more.

And on two bookcases, all their own, were the clockwork masterpieces: a row of ducks, a monkey and an organ grinder, a little drummer boy, a few perfect locomotives, carousels upon carousels, a cat playing a fiddle, to name but a few. Toys so beautiful and perfect that Fiona could not breathe, all she could do was gasp.

"You made… all of these?" she whispered, like speaking too loudly might shatter the magic of this secret workshop, tucked away down an Old Town passage.

Her father turned and smiled. "Do ye like them?"

"Like them? I am almost jealous of all the bairns who get them!"

He chuckled. "I've made a fair few for ye over the years."

"You have?" She frowned, trying to remember.

"That rabbit that pops out of the cabbage—that's one of mine. One of me finest, actually," he told her, her eyes widening further.

"You said you bought it for me!"

He shrugged. "A wee lie. That dolly ye used to love when ye were four or so was the first thing I ever made. Gave me the idea for all of this," he swept his arm around, "if truth be told. I was just startin' to make a fair wage at Mr. Walker's, and we'd nae long moved into our apartments, so there wasnae much coin to spare. I made that dolly for ye, and then I thought—how many other wee lassies and laddies willnae have aught to cheer them this Christmas? It was many years before I began this, o' course, but that's where the thought started."

Just then, three knocks thudded at the low-lintelled door, startling Fiona. She hurried to the safety of her father, and not a moment too soon, for a giant bear of a man swung the door wide and strode in without permission. He loomed in the doorway, the lantern light making him appear like a monster, thick-set and enormous, with a coarse red beard and one milky eye that glinted in the dim. A mane of wild red hair could not be restrained beneath a cloth cap, springing out wherever it pleased.

He cupped his hands to his mouth and blew into them, stomping the snow off his boots and peeling off his oilskin coat, hanging it up on a hook. "Bloody cold enough to freeze the bollocks of a brass monkey out there," he growled, one bushy eyebrow shooting up as he looked at Fiona. "Who's this, then?"

"Me daughter, Fiona. I told ye I'd be bringin' her so put the kettle on to boil and stop scarin' the poor lass," Donal replied, chuckling as he put an arm around Fiona's shoulders. "Tommy here is an old friend of mine. A good friend. He protects this workshop when I'm nae here and protects *me* when I make me rounds through the Old Town on Christmas night."

"Aye, and for me tireless work, I get first pick of what he makes for me own bairns," Tommy said, still blowing on his hands as he went to the tiny woodstove in the far corner of the room, setting to the task of stoking a fire. There were some embers still aglow, suggesting someone had been there earlier in the night. Tommy, Fiona presumed.

Fiona rallied her nerves. "You have children?"

"Two lads, two lasses. Apples of me eye." Tommy smiled, his teeth surprising white and straight. "They look forward to one of yer da's clockwork toys every year. I'd have me arse whipped if I went home without one for each!"

Donal clicked his tongue. "Mind yer language around me daughter."

"Aye, sorry." Tommy laughed. "I'm nae used to havin' anyone here but yer da. She didnae inherit yer brogue, then?"

Donal shook his head, smiling. "Fortunately, nay. She sounds every bit like her ma."

"Have you met my mama?" Fiona squinted at the huge man, uncertain if it was the surrounding of toys or the lantern light or the fact that he had children, but he was beginning to look less frightening.

Tommy stood up, admiring the makings of a good fire. "Nay, I cannae say I have. Yer da keeps his Old Town life and New Town life separate, and I daenae blame him. This isnae any place for a lass like that." He paused, seemingly realising what he had said. "Nae that there's anythin' scary out there, nae on Christmas. At Christmas, everyone is safe and happy. That's the rules. That's the magic."

Fiona mulled over the big man's words for a while, her innocent mind finding the perfect sense in what he was saying. She had thought the same thing herself while feasting and watching the snow with her parents—no one could be suffering when the world was filled with winter magic. It simply was not possible.

"What about when it's not Christmas?" she asked.

Tommy shrugged. "Folk get by, as they've always done and always will."

She did not quite understand what that meant and had no chance to consider it as her father clapped his hands together and announced, "Come on, then! We've nay time to be wastin'. Let's get these toys in the sacks and see if we cannae create some of that magic ourselves, eh?" He flashed a pointed look at Tommy. "Ye get that tea boilin'. We ought to have somethin' warm before we head out."

How will that help us when we're outside? Fiona was not sure, nor was she sure why her father was suddenly so obsessed with tea, but she was too excited to think any more about it. She ran to the workbench and hopped up on a shabby stool, where her father handed her a vast canvas sack.

"Ye see them sheets of newspaper there?" Donal nodded to three towering stacks of old newspaper, almost as tall as the stool.

Fiona nodded.

"I'll put the toys on the bench, ye wrap 'em in a sheet of newspaper apiece, then Tommy over there will put 'em in the sacks. We'll have sacks for laddies and sacks for lassies, aye?" Donal smiled. "Ye make sure ye ken which sack is which, and make sure ye wrap 'em up nice and tight."

Fiona's heart leapt with joy. "I will, Papa."

"That's me wee ducklin'."

Steadfast in her duties, Fiona set to work, diligently folding each beautiful, painstakingly made toy into what she thought was rather meagre wrapping, learning quickly which toys could be rolled, with the ends twisted, and which had to be more carefully folded into their newspaper jackets. And after each toy was wrapped, she placed it gently at the end of the table, where Tommy was waiting to put everything into the large canvas sacks that pooled on the ground by his feet.

She worried for the dolls and the clockwork and the nutcrackers, fearful that they might be damaged, being all stuffed together like that, but Tommy assured her that the toys were tougher than they looked.

"They come alive in the shop, ye ken," Tommy teased, pausing in his sack duties to pour three cups of steaming, hot tea.

Fiona cast him a withering look. "They do not."

"They do, but ye have to be stealthy, else they'll pretend they were nae up to nay good," Tommy insisted, grinning. "I've found the dolls havin' a tea party by the woodstove more than a few times, and I've found the nutcrackers standin' guard by the door when I've nipped out to fetch somethin'. Och, and I had the fright of me life when that drummer boy started bangin' on his drums while I had me back turned!"

Fiona pursed her lips, pensive. "You're jesting with me."

"Maybe." Tommy chuckled. "Maybe nae. But I like to think the dolls, the ducks, the frogs, all of 'em keep a few children company when they need it."

On that, Fiona could agree, for she had often relied on the company of her own dolls and toys when her mother was out or when the girls at school had been unkind to her. Even at night, when her mother and father were in their bedchamber and she was in hers, feeling a little lonely in the dark, she always felt better just by glancing at her beloved toys, watching over her as she slept. Perhaps, these toys would be a guardian for someone like her, who felt a little lonely and maybe a little scared.

Bring your magic to them, she wished silently. *Even if Tommy is fibbing, keep your new children company. Watch over them.*

She sipped her hot tea and cradled her hands around the cup in between wrapping the rest of the toys, to stop her ink-blackened fingers turning numb. It was bitingly cold in the workshop, the small woodstove barely coughing out enough warmth to keep a mouse from freezing.

"I hope Mama keeps the fire going for when we get home," she said as she worked. "I don't think I want to be this cold, ever again."

When her father and Tommy said nothing in reply, she looked up, and found them staring at one another, both wearing the same painfully sad expression, as if she had said something wrong. Not wanting to find out what it was she had said to upset them, she returned to her work, pretending she had not spoken at all.

Chapter Three

The beautiful snow had decided to turn vengeful by the time that Fiona, her father, and Tommy left the workshop with the first sacks thrown over their shoulders.

The plan was to return for the rest once they ran out of what they had, though Fiona was convinced she had been given a lighter load. The sacks that her father and Tommy were carrying bent their backs, as if they were walking through a powerful wind, while she barely struggled.

Through the haze of white that stung at her face, Fiona could not see a thing, though shadows and shapes shifted through the snowstorm, appearing and disappearing, chilling her far more than the snow itself ever could. But her father stayed at her side, presumably so she would not lose her way... or so no one would snatch her.

"Right, this is where we'll start," Donal announced, pausing at the top of a grim street, an old sign reading 'Cowgate.'

Fiona frowned.

Even without the veil of white, she would not have known where the lodgings were, for though there were occasional doors, she could not tell if the rows of dark stone belonged to houses or lodgings or if it was one enormous residence. A few stubby candles flickered at sooty windows, while strange sounds drifted through the dark: wailing, screaming, bellowing, and the shrill cry of babies.

I want to go home, she knew, her heart pounding. But if she asked her father to take her, she feared he might be disappointed. Indeed, he might not believe her when she had said she wanted to help others. Perhaps, helping others was harder than she had realised.

"Just stay back with Tommy for the first few," her father said. "See how it works, and then ye can start handin' out what ye've brought."

Fiona nodded, too nervous to speak.

Her father approached the first door, which appeared to be hanging half off its hinges. It swung open and a glassy-eyed man answered. He did not wear a shirt, his skin streaked in dirt and grime, his trousers stained and threadbare. He wore no shoes, his feet black and missing several toenails.

"What?" he grumbled, his voice faraway.

"It's Father Christmas," Donal replied with a smile. "Toys for the bairns."

The man turned back into the gloomy hallway behind him, where a rickety staircase climbed up into a drafty, cobwebbed realm. More noise wafted down, sounds of sorrow and pain that brought sudden, strange tears to Fiona's eyes.

"Lizzie!" the man barked. "Father Christmas is 'ere!"

A door opened somewhere in the grim of the hallway, and hurried footsteps announced the arrival of Lizzie. She was young and pretty, her face flushed as if she had not long been tending to a pot, but even she could not escape the filth; it blotted her plump cheeks, and had turned what might once have been a white dress into something grey and worn.

"We prayed ye were comin'!" Lizzie cheered, pushing past the glassy-eyed man. "Get back into the room and put a shirt on," she told him as he shambled off, knocking into the walls on his way. "And daenae wake the bairns. I want 'em to be surprised in the mornin'."

Donal smiled. "Ye look well, Lizzie."

"Och, well enough." She beamed back. "Even better now ye're here. Ye're a wonder, sir. Every year, I worry ye willnae be comin', every year ye come."

Donal opened the sack, giving her the pick of the gifts. "This is for lassies. Me big, grizzled helper here has the ones for the laddies."

Tommy stepped forward, opening the sack, and Fiona could not help but join him, standing awkwardly as she observed the world beyond that broken door.

It was as if she had been living in heaven, in her grand apartments in the New Town, and these people had found themselves in some sort of Hell on Earth.

It was colder inside, somehow, than it was out in the street, and the walls were covered in blooming mould, a damp smell permeating.

Though there were other, worse smells beneath that earthy aroma. And so much noise. Noise that surely made it impossible for anyone to sleep, though Lizzie had mentioned her children being asleep.

How is it possible that she has children? Fiona could not fathom it, for Lizzie barely seemed older than her.

"Thank ye, lads," Lizzie said, dipping into the sacks until she had three from the boys' bag and two from the girls'. "I daenae even want to ken what's in 'em, so it'll be a surprise for me too!"

Donal chuckled. "Och, ye'll peek. Ye willnae be able to help it."

"Aye, maybe." Lizzie cradled the newspaper-wrapped gifts in her arms and chinned up at the staircase. "I'll just put these by the fireplace, then I'll go knockin' for ye. Daenae want ye riskin' them stairs with those sacks."

"Still nae fixed?" Tommy asked.

Lizzie shook her head sadly. "Doubt they'll be fixed 'til they crumble. Even then, we'll just end up with a couple of ladders." She smiled. "But it's Christmas—let's nae speak of crumblin' stairs."

She hurried back down the hallway, reappearing a few moments later, rapping on the doors of the ground floor before bounding up the staircase, the thud of her knuckles echoing up and up to what must have been the eaves of the place. So many people, crammed into one building.

Yet, nothing could have prepared Fiona for the flood of mothers that came to the front door, not at all matching the number of knocks that Lizzie had made.

There must've been a hundred, all lining up neatly, snaking up the staircase and landings, whispering excitedly.

"Where did they all come from?" Fiona whispered, tugging on Tommy's sleeve.

Tommy peered down at her. "What do ye mean?"

"There are… too many."

He nodded his head in understanding. "There's twenty or so rooms in here, and some of 'em will have four or five families in a room. Lizzie and her husband keep everythin' in order, more or less, so they get a room to themselves."

"But that's… too many!" Fiona repeated in a whisper, her eyes so wide she feared the icy wind might freeze them that way.

Tommy patted her gently on the shoulder. "Aye, but people make do, as they've always done. It's nae pretty, but it's how folk survive." He chinned toward Lizzie. "Some of 'em make the best of it, some of 'em just… do what they can. Ye just watch and listen, and see if it doesnae turn that shock into somethin' softer."

Fiona did as she had been asked, concentrating on her father and the rapport he seemed to have with the excited mothers who came forward to take their turn, dipping into the sacks as if the gifts were for them.

"Me wee Nathan hasnae stopped playin' with that horse since last year," one of the women said, clasping her hands as if in prayer. "Loves it more than he's ever loved anythin', but he's been wantin' a soldier to go with it. Do ye think ye have a soldier he could have? He's nae been the same since his da died. I think it'd cheer him."

Donal searched through the sack, coming up with just the thing. "See if this cannae make him smile, eh?" He passed the gift over and the woman, for a moment, looked like she might cry.

"Thank ye, Father Christmas," she choked with a wink. "Ye daenae ken what this night means for us."

"Ye just take care of yerselves, d'ye hear?" Donal urged.

The woman nodded and moved aside for the next mother. And as the line grew smaller, Fiona realised that every mother had a sad story—deaths, sicknesses, injuries, husbands in jail, husbands running off, children dying, lost employment, no employment, no money for wood or coal to warm themselves. It did not end, the spool of misery, and yet the women were all smiling and thanking Donal, clutching the newspaper-wrapped gifts as if they were the Crown Jewels themselves, telling him how that one little present would make the entire year seem less awful: a balm to soothe the pain of their everyday existence.

"The lasses were heartbroken when the dolls ended up as firewood. They'll be talkin' about this for weeks!" one said.

"There's peace in the streets 'cause of ye, Father Christmas. All the bairns out there, playin' with one another—nay one jealous of the other. Warms me heart every bloody year!" said another.

"I might see me wee lad smile again," wept a third.

A fourth held tight to three gifts. "Ye make it feel like a different sort of day, ye ken?"

Soon enough, they were at the last mother, who stepped forward with an ashen face, her eyes brimming with tears. Her fingers shook violently as she reached to take Donal's hand, gripping it so tight that her knuckles whitened.

"Can I… still have one?" she asked, her voice cracking. "I lost wee Bessie last month. She was… beggin' me for her dolly at… the end. I couldnae tell her I'd used it… for the fire. I ken I daenae… have a bairn anymore, but… do ye think I could have one for her? To put where she's… buried?"

Fiona had to turn away, a sob shaking her shoulders. Tommy put an arm around her, pulling her against his side so she could weep into his thick oilskin coat. He smelled of tobacco and woodsmoke, a comforting scent. And she clung to him, her heart hurting for the people of the Old Town. People she had been afraid of. People she had wanted to run from, to return to her warm apartments in the New Town.

"Of course," Donal said softly. "Of course ye can. Here, let me find ye a dolly. What colour hair?"

"Red," the woman wheezed, her own sobs setting off a new round in Fiona.

There was a rustle of paper, and the cracked sound of someone breaking, a whimper so devastating that Fiona could not breathe.

"Thank ye," the woman whispered. "Thank ye, from the bottom of me heart."

"Ye daenae need to thank me," Donal told her. "Ye take this to yer lass and ye wish her a Merry Christmas and I'll say a prayer for her, too."

Fiona saw her father embrace the poor woman, and though that might have repulsed her a short while ago, wondering how her father could bear to hug all of that filth and unpleasantness, she suddenly wanted to hug the woman herself. So, she pulled away from Tommy and went to the woman, putting her arms around her waist.

"Merry Christmas," Fiona whispered. "I'm sorry."

The woman clung onto her, sobbing into Fiona's shoulder. "Oh, sweet lass. Thank ye. Thank ye. Merry... Christmas to ye." She sucked in a shaky breath. "It's like holdin' her again. Och, thank ye. This is... the gift I needed. This is... the gift."

Before long, the woman's sobs eased, and she pulled away from Fiona with a smile, cradling the wooden doll in her arm. The woman put a tender hand to Fiona's cheek for a moment, before stepping back. "Ye be on yer way now," she said. "There'll be more families in need of ye tonight. Merry Christmas."

"Merry Christmas," Fiona, Donal, and Tommy chorused, as the woman nodded and closed the door, signalling the end of their first stop of the night.

And as Fiona thought of the morning, when those children would wake up to toys and gifts, she smiled across at her father and understood: he was a hero amongst these people, and he was passing on the brutal beauty of it to her, opening her eyes to all of the things she had been sheltered from.

"Shall we?" she said, swinging her sack up onto her shoulder.

Her father grinned. "Aye. Onward!"

Chapter Four

After two return journeys to the workshop to retrieve more toys, it seemed to Fiona like the trio had given gifts to all of Edinburgh, yet she was not tired at all. Her bones and limbs might have been frozen solid, but her heart was as warm as a furnace. The stories of the people of the Old Town had not been any happier, and she doubted she would forget a single one, but the fact that such a small offering of joy could turn misery into hope, even just for one day, allowed her heart to feel full, her soul gladdened.

"I never knew it was like this," Fiona waxed enthusiastic, holding onto her father's hand. "And you do this tomorrow as well?"

Donal nodded. "If there're toys left."

"I wish I could see their faces," she cooed. "Don't you ever want to see their faces?"

Donal shrugged. "That's for the mas and das, nae for me. That's what they deserve, ye ken?"

"I think so," Fiona replied, though she did not really. She would have given anything to see the children's reactions.

Heading back to the curving cobbles of Cockburn Street with half-empty sacks, so they could wander the farthest reaches of the Old Town without running out, they were about to cut through the passageway where the workshop hid, when shadows appeared in the blizzard that had yet to feel festive enough to ebb back into a slow drift of flakes. Fiona squinted, wondering if she was seeing things.

She tugged on her father's hand. "I think someone is there."

"Hmm?" Her father squinted at the silhouetted shapes... and his face paled.

The shapes became flesh, four thick-set men striding out of the snowstorm, faces grim, eyes dark, their intent unknown but certainly not good.

"Well, well, if it's nae Father Christmas and his wee helpers," one of the men, head shaven, said.

Another smirked. "Aye, we been waitin' for ye."

"Thought we'd help ye with yer charity," laughed a fourth, drawing swollen hands out of deep pockets.

Tommy immediately stepped in front of Fiona, putting an arm across her. Meanwhile, her father closed ranks, blocking her from the view of those gruff and grizzled men. But she did not need to see them to know that these were people her father had encountered before. It had been obvious in the way that Donal's face had completely drained of blood.

"Run," her father whispered.

Tommy peered down at her. "Aye, run. Now."

She hesitated, her mouth half-open in protest, but Tommy subtly shook his head and gave her a firm push in the chest, as if to say, "don't argue, just go." The trouble was, she did not know where to go. She glanced at the passageway where the workshop was waiting, brimming with toys that the children of Old Town deserved more than anything.

Tommy gave her another, harder shove that almost knocked her over. Holding her balance, she realised she had to obey, for if her father and Tommy were frightened, this was no place for her. Taking off, she darted down the passageway, sprinting right past the workshop, hurtling on, doing her best not to trip and fall in the swallowing darkness.

She knew there was another end to the passageway somewhere, and all she had to do was reach it. From there, she did not know what she would do or where she would go, but the passageway was no longer safe.

Up ahead, her unaccustomed eyes caught a glimpse of white—the snow guiding her to some semblance of sanctuary. Forcing her frozen limbs to keep moving, she did not dare to look back, terrified of what she might see or hear. She concentrated solely on the thud of her boots against the ground and the rush of blood in her ears.

Almost there, she told herself. *Almost there. Then, we'll find our way home. Papa will catch up to me. All will be well. It's Christmas—all* has *to be well.*

The arch of white was no more than twenty paces away, when something yanked hard on her hand. The jerk of it nearly sent her sprawling, but something solid caught her and dragged her down, breaking her fall but denying her freedom. She opened her mouth, willing a scream to burst out of her dry throat, but a hand closed over it. Meanwhile, a thin but strong arm snaked around her neck, pulling her deeper into an unknown darkness. She felt the scrape of something against her coat, snagging the wool, and a meaty, earthy smell filled her nostrils.

Is this what it feels like to be buried alive? her mind wondered strangely, her heart fluttering wildly in her chest, her stomach twisting into knots. Something bad was about to happen, something worse than what would have faced her if she had stayed with her father; she just did not know what that bad thing was yet. Perhaps, there had been a fifth man, lying in wait to block the passageway. Perhaps, he had caught her.

"Get that lass!" a loud bellow rang in her ears, her hot breath steaming against a rough, unfamiliar palm. "Daenae let her escape! She'll send for the constables!"

Footsteps thundered down the passage, matching the racing beat of her heart, and though there was no light to see by, her hearing compensated. She could feel the man approaching, hear him getting closer and closer, until he was almost upon the dank spot where she had been dragged. No doubt, the thug who had caught her would make himself known, telling his associate not to bother, that the task had already been achieved.

But all she heard was quiet breathing behind her, and the continued stampede of her pursuer. She squeezed her eyes shut as the footfalls pounded right in front of her... and then carried on, straight past her.

Still, her captor did not release her, that hand remaining tight across her mouth. But why had they not called to the man running by? Why had they not revealed her whereabouts? Why had they dragged her into the dark like that, whoever they were?

What do they mean to do with me? She kept her eyes closed, bracing for the worst.

At length, the owner of the hand slowly began to loosen their grip, withdrawing their arm from around her neck first, before gingerly removing their hand.

"Daenae scream or yell," a surprisingly soft voice said. "We daenae ken if they've gone, and I daenae want 'em comin' back for ye. They've been waitin' there for hours."

Fiona caught her breath, clasping a hand to her chest. "What did you grab me like that for?" It seemed like the obvious question. "Who are you?"

She heard someone scrabbling around, followed by the hissing strike of a match. A small flame burst into life, spreading its glow to the wick of a stubby candle. In the smoky light, she saw an urchin staring back at her. A boy with a shock of black hair, his face smeared with dirt, his lower lip split and scabbed, and one bright blue eye swollen up as though recently punched.

He shrugged, flashing a shy smile. "I was tryin' to help ye. Like I said, them men have been waitin' for a fair while for ye and yer da to come back. Been waitin' since just after the last time ye came back for more... uh... of whatever ye have in them sacks."

Thinking of the sack she still had in her hands, she wrapped her arms around it, hugging it to her protectively.

"Ye *are* the toy man's daughter, aye?" the boy asked, touching his split lip and wincing.

"That's no concern of yours." She frowned. "Where are we?"

Wooden slats surrounded them on three sides, like they were in the middle of a giant crate, all covered over in some kind of black material. A tarpaulin or oilskins or something of that ilk. And behind her, the mismatched stone of the passageway wall. The space was narrow, only just fitting the two of them inside.

"Home," the boy said simply. "For now, anyway, 'til I get moved on. Been here a few weeks. I'm Alastair."

She frowned at him. "And you… saved me?"

"I suppose so." He shrugged. "Just didnae want ye gettin' hurt. I ken those men. They're nae good people. They'd have caught ye if ye'd kept runnin'. So, are ye the toy man's daughter? That fella who goes round the houses and gives out toys?"

She hesitated, before nodding and hugging the sack tighter to her chest.

"Can I help ye?" he asked.

"Help me?"

He scratched his filthy hair. "Aye. I've seen yer da every year since I was a wee bairn. Always wanted to offer me services, but never had the nerve." He paused. "Ye have to finish givin' out them toys. If ye tell me where ye were headed, I can help."

"I have to wait for my father," she insisted. "He told me to run, but he won't be able to find me if I don't stay close by."

The boy rested his hand on her arm. "Stay here. I'll see if they're still out there. Them lads and yer da."

Before she could argue, he shot out of his crate hideaway, though she could barely hear his footsteps as he made his way down the passageway.

Too scared to follow him, she shuffled closer to the candle and brought her palms up to the flame, as close as she dared without getting burnt, letting the feeble warmth bring some feeling back into her numb fingers.

A few minutes later, her heart jumped into her throat as the black fabric was thrown back and Alastair scuttled inside, sliding onto his skinned knees. "Nay one there." He offered an apologetic look. "If yer da and his pal have any sense, they'll have run too."

"Run?" Fiona's stomach lurched. "Without me?"

The boy hesitated. "I can take ye back to wherever ye live, if ye like? But… I really think ye ought to keep givin' out them toys." He sounded oddly nervous, his fingertips lightly caressing the sack of toys as if it contained precious diamonds. "There's a lot of bairns who'll be lookin' forward to openin' 'em tomorrow mornin'. And I really can help. Tell me what street ye were at, and I can carry on with ye."

Fiona sat there in silence, utterly torn.

She did not want to continue without her father, she did not want to think about where her father might be, but nor did she want to disappoint the children who were hoping to have something to treasure when dawn rose.

It did not seem fair that some would have gifts, and some would go without, when she had not been captured and she still had toys to deliver, and she had someone right beside her who was willing to help. He did not seem like a thief; if he was, he would have taken the sack already. And he *did* seem very anxious to assist her.

"Will you... help me get home afterwards?" she asked quietly. "If my father had to run, that's where he'll be. And I think he'd like it if I finished what he started tonight. I think... he'd be proud of me."

More than anything, she hoped it would be enough to distract her from what might have happened to her father and Tommy. If she could put smiles on people's faces and hear their stories, then things might not feel so bad.

And then, she would return to her apartments in the New Town, find her father waiting there, and she would be able to regale him with the story of how she had completed his Christmas mission, so he did not have to worry about it.

"Aye, I'll take ye wherever ye need to go, after we've delivered them toys," Alistair said, brightening.

Fiona shrugged. "Then, we should go while those awful men are gone. They might come back." She hesitated. "But I should fetch something first. Can you stand guard?"

"From the workshop? Aye, I'll watch the entrance," he replied, startling her.

"You know about the workshop?"

He blinked, his cheeks turning red in the low light. "I've been... uh... watchin' yer da for a while. Kept waitin' for me chance to offer help, like I told ye." He smiled. "Seems like this is the night, eh?"

"You'd better not try to steal anything," she scolded, trying to sound authoritative. "You can have a toy at the end, once we've delivered everything else. You can pick which one you want, I suppose, but... don't steal anything."

He stared at her, his expression outraged. "I wouldnae steal anythin'. If I wanted to, I'd have done it ages ago."

"That's what I thought," she mumbled, clambering out of the hiding place. "Well, come on then. There's no time to waste. The sun will be up soon enough."

Alastair hurried after her. "I'll nae let ye down!"

As she tentatively edged back down the passageway towards the workshop, she prayed that she was not making a very grave mistake, dragged out of one dangerous situation only to be thrown into another.

Chapter Five

The residents of the Old Town seemed surprised to find a twelve-year-old girl and a street urchin with a swollen eye, a split lip, and bare feet at their doors. Distrust gleamed in the narrowed eyes of those who answered her knock, their gazes darting left and right, as if expecting some terrible attack instead of a gift.

"I know I'm not who you're expecting," Fiona fumbled to say, her nerves tightening her throat, "but I'm the daughter of the… um… Father Christmas who comes here each year. He's poorly, you see, and I didn't want the bairns to be without toys for Christmas, so I said I'd do his work for him."

The first woman they encountered only glared harder. "Ye speak strange. Are ye nae from Scotland, lass?"

"I am!" Fiona insisted. "I was born and bred here, Ma'am. My father is the one who delivers presents. Please, I just want to continue his work whilst he's not feeling well. Next year, I'm sure it'll be him again. I beg of you, let me finish his work tonight."

Please, let it be him again, she prayed in desperation, her stomach dropping as she thought of all the awful things that might have befallen her father. He might be in a ditch at that very moment or bleeding in the middle of the road, buried beneath a blanket of falling snow like the drunkards in the park. All the way back to the place where she, her father, and Tommy had left off, she had wondered if she was doing the right thing, or if she would be better served in searching for her father.

"It willnae do ye any good," Alastair had insisted. *"Ye'll nae find him in a blizzard like this, and if he's run off, he'll nae dare to come back here for a few hours, in case them lads are waitin' again."*

The rake thin woman at the door seemed to soften, perhaps seeing Fiona's distress. "Ye truly are his daughter."

Fiona was not certain if it was a question, so she nodded, murmuring, "I am. I swear, I am. I just want to do some good."

As soon as she opened the sack of toys, the woman's expression softened further, tears brimming in her eyes. "Och, me bairns are all grown now, with bairns of their own, but I'll call the other lasses down for their pick. Ye just wait there. I'll see if I've a nip of somethin' too—ye look half frozen, out in this snow." She laughed. "I suppose I should've believed ye from the start, considerin' nay miscreant would be out in this willingly."

Mothers and fathers alike came down to select wrapped toys for their children, and the first woman seemed to have passed the message on that there were two shivering children doing the delivering, as those in line began to offer something small in exchange for the gifts a chunk of bread, a sliver of a pie, a piece of cheese, a nip of something potent, a hot cup of tea for them to warm their hands on for a while. Some even invited Fiona and Alastair inside to sit by the fire, but Fiona refused politely.

"We've to get the rest of these delivered by sunrise," she explained, thanking them profusely for their kindness. She even tried to give back the offerings, the thought of taking them making her feel guilty, but as they insisted, Alastair whispered something in her ear.

"Ye'll offend them if ye daenae take *their* gifts. These are proud people."

So, Fiona accepted the gifts with a smile and with thanks, until there was no one left in the line but the first woman they had spoken with.

"Ye take care of yerselves," the woman said. "And if ye do need a warm fire to sit by when ye're done, ye come on by again. Ye're welcome here."

Fiona took the woman's hands in hers, a look of understanding passing between the pair, and as they bid one another farewell, Fiona could not help but feel as the magic in the air. With every door she knocked on, every story she heard, every person she spoke with, she felt more and more glad that she had chosen to carry on, despite not knowing where her father was. The night was changing her, and she knew that when she *did* return to her apartments in the New Town, she would never be the same again.

"They shared what they couldn't afford to share," Fiona whispered, more to herself than to Alastair, who did not seem to feel the cold at all. "They would've given me the coat off their backs."

Alastair smiled. "We daenae have much here, but we're richer in other ways than ye fancy folks over the other side of the park."

"Couldn't you find shelter somewhere here?" Fiona asked, worried for the boy at her side. After all, while she would eventually be going home, he would presumably be returning to his house of crates, with nothing but a small candle to keep him warm.

Alastair's smile dimmed. "I like where I am. Nay one bothers me there."

"But how do you not freeze to death in winter?"

He shrugged. "I'm tough as old boots, me." He took hold of her hand, his grin returning as he led her further down the street. "Anyway, forget about me. Ye're dawdlin'! We've got too much to do!"

She could not help but laugh at his enthusiasm, enjoying the boundless cheer of the boy who had nothing yet desperately wanted to give out toys to the children of the Old Town. *He* was like magic: a force of festive spirit to keep her going through the blizzard and the unknown fate of her father.

"Keep yer hat on, I'm coming!" she replied, letting him guide her to the next door.

***

Just as dawn was about to break, the snow finally decided to relent, sending downy feathers from the still-swollen heavens to grace the cheeks of the two children who had spent all night giving out toys.

They had gone back and forth to the workshop until there was nothing left on the shelves or bookcases, Fiona perpetually hoping that she would find her father there during one of their journeys. But he had not returned. Nor had Tommy. And she had been forced to swallow the bad feeling that something truly wretched had taken place, saving her panic for when the job was done.

She could not have done any of it without Alastair. The unlikely friend who should, by rights, have stolen the toys and sold them to make his life more comfortable, yet seemed entirely satisfied every time another toy was handed out. The act itself warmed him, somehow, for he had not complained or suffered in the bitter weather, though he had walked the whole night through in a too-big shirt that revealed his bare, pigeon chest, a threadbare bit of cloth that might once have been a cloak, trousers that were too small and ripped all over, and no shoes to speak of.

"Do ye think they're openin' the presents now?" Alastair asked, his blue eyes bright and eager, as he swung his empty sack back and forth.

Fiona smiled shyly at him. "I think it might be too early yet. I don't open my presents until eight o'clock."

"Do ye have a tree?" His eyes widened further, slipping his hand into hers and squeezing it tight.

The touch startled Fiona for a moment, but his hand was like a block of ice, the cold seeping through the wool of her gloves. She gripped his hand in return, hoping to feed some heat into his.

"We have a small one," Fiona admitted, somewhat guiltily.

He seemed to swoon for a moment, dancing a little jig. "Do ye get to light the candles on it? Do ye put ribbons on it? Or them bauble things I've heard about—those colourful glass ball things?"

"We just have one bauble," Fiona replied. "A German client of my father's gave it to him about two Christmases ago, in return for some work he did."

Alastair nodded effusively. "When I'm older, I'm goin' to have a tree with candles and ribbons and baubles and everythin' ye could ever want to put on a Christmas tree. And I'm goin' to have a feast on Christmas Day, and I'll invite everyone I ken!"

"Would you invite me?" Fiona blushed a little, despite the cold.

He stared at her for a moment, deciding. "Aye, I'd invite ye. Why would I nae? Ye're the lass that's given me the best Christmas Eve of me life!" He paused. "Second best, maybe."

"What was the first?"

He threw the sack over his shoulders, wearing it like a cloak, and lifted his shoulders in a half shrug. "Was a few years back. Just a... normal Christmas Eve. Had me first mince pie. We had this little cluster of twigs that me ma made to look like a tree, and I made somethin' for her and put it under the tree. We sat in front of the fire with me da and sang carols. That was maybe me favourite."

"That sounds nice," Fiona said, meaning it. It made her miss her own mother, who would undoubtedly be worried sick, and for good reason. "Where *are* your ma and pa?"

Alastair shook his head, saying nothing. And after the stories she had heard that night, Fiona knew better than to press him for a reply.

A short while later, just as they reached the crossroads where the Royal Mile met Cockburn Street, he spoke again. "Thank ye for lettin' me help ye tonight. I ken ye probably didnae want to trust me, but thank ye for trustin' me anyway. I really did just want to help."

"I can see that now," she told him, lifting his hand to her mouth, blowing hot air onto the icy skin. "I think you might love Christmas more than my father."

He blinked at the kind gesture, put did not pull his hand away. "I sit by the kirkyard sometimes, listenin' to the carols and hymns. Feels like… I daenae ken what it feels like, but it's… a warmness."

"Magic," she said. "It feels like magic."

He nodded slowly. "Aye, maybe that's it. Magic."

They made their way down Cockburn Street, cutting left into the passageway. At the workshop door, Fiona's heart lurched. It was ajar, and she was certain she had closed it behind her during their last journey to stock the sacks.

All of the worst possibilities struck her first, wondering if those thugs had found the workshop in an attempt to pillage it, ransacking it when they found there was nothing left.

But then, she heard a voice. A familiar voice.

"I'll head back when it gets light," her father said. "She'll be home safe with her ma, so daenae fret. I'm nae leavin' ye here like this."

Giddy with relief, Fiona burst through the door to find Tommy lying on the ground by the woodstove and her father sitting beside him on a milking stool, wrapping the bigger man's bleeding leg in bandages. Her father looked unscathed, but Tommy had clearly faced a fight with those thugs; his face was a mess of bruises and cuts and swelling, his knuckles a dark purple.

"Ducklin'!" her father yelped, jumping up. "What are ye doin' here? Why are ye nae at home?"

"Papa, you're not going to believe me, but—" Fiona turned to introduce Alastair, to tell the story of what they had done together, but the boy was gone. Puzzled, she ran back out into the passageway, her head whipping left and right in search of him. She even went to his hiding place of broken crates and black tarpaulin, peering into the gloom, but the candle had gone and so had he.

"What are ye doin', ducklin'? Get back into the warmth and tell me where on Earth ye've been!" her father called from the door of the workshop.

She wandered past him to the passageway entrance, scouring the snowy ground for Alastair's footsteps in the fresh snow, but the falling flakes and the icy wind had whipped them away already, as if he had never existed at all.

Chapter Six

Edinburgh, 1860

"Shall we have some roasted chestnuts?" Beryl asked, weaving her arm through Fiona's.

Fiona beamed up at her mother. "From that man on the corner of the bridge? He always has the best ones."

"Oh, he does! Yes, let's get some from him to warm ourselves, and then I thought we might go to that tea shop you like. We should rest our legs after all this walking." Beryl was in fine, festive spirits, and the feeling was mutual for Fiona.

The first snow had been late in falling, but Fiona could scent it in the air, the thick clouds gathering on the horizon, framing the gothic beauty of the city's constant sentinel, perched high above the old and the new: Edinburgh Castle.

They made their slow, casual way along the edge of Princes Street Gardens, leaning into one another, enjoying the simple pleasure of being in each other's company on a cold winter day.

They had spent most of the morning in the shops of the New Town, trying to find something appropriate for Fiona to wear for her "very important meeting" next week, set to take place just a few days after Christmas.

It was only in the last dressmakers that they had found the perfect gown—a Bertha, low on the shoulders, made of brushed lilac silk, with the most exquisite Honiton lace flounce, draping the dramatic neckline.

She had even agreed to her first crinoline, after the lady in the shop had shown her what the silhouette would look like. Indeed, at six-and-ten, it was the most beautiful she had ever felt.

"Will I be allowed to spend Christmas with you, when I'm married?" Fiona asked suddenly, realising the enormity of what next week's meeting might mean, if all went well. "Am I expected to spend Christmas with his family, or are we supposed to have our own Christmas? I... hadn't thought about that."

Beryl pressed a kiss to her daughter's hair. "You can do all those things. Of course, it's customary for you to be with his family on Christmas Day, but it won't interrupt our "Yule" celebrations." She flashed a wink at Fiona. "The 21st will always be ours, my darling."

"But what about... you know." Fiona nudged her mother lightly in the ribs. "How will I explain that? Should I... lie? I suppose I could say that I want to spend my Christmas Eves with you, and then pretend I didn't sleep well."

Beryl gazed ahead, furrowing her brow. "You might have to... stop for a while. Or, perhaps, you can help your father every other year. It depends what Kelvin's nature is like. You might find you want to share the secret with him, if he's a charitable sort of man. He might even offer to help. But that will take time to figure out, so I think next year you might have to let your father do his Christmas duties alone."

"Oh..." Fiona looked toward the weather-stained buildings across the park; the crooked homes built on steep slopes, winding in a labyrinth that, in the daylight, did not look so dismal. There was beauty over the other side of the gardens that split the city, beauty that Fiona held dear, especially at that time of year.

I'll find a way, she told herself, refusing to let her mood dampen. It was almost Christmas, there was a grand tree in the middle of the park, the shops were all decorated, the air was filled with the sweet scent of roasting chestnuts and mulled wine, children were singing carols around the base of the exquisite, spired Scott Monument, and she had excellent prospects arranged for her, to secure a comfortable future — what right did she have to be maudlin, when she had so much to be grateful for?

"Kelvin is from a good family," her mother continued. "I'm certain he'll be the sort of fellow who'll champion your charitable work. And if not, then... maybe we *will* tell a few little lies so you can carry on. I know how much Christmas Eve means to you."

Fiona smiled at her mother. "Thank you." She paused, pulling a face. "Does this mean I'm going to have to learn to cook? I'm not sure Kelvin knows what he's got ahead of him, if this meeting goes well. Do you remember that poor chicken?"

"Singed to a crisp," her mother chuckled. "But when I first married your father, I couldn't boil an egg. Couldn't do anything with an egg. I... made countless mistakes, burned a lot of things, but I learned. Besides, I don't think you'll have to worry—you'll have staff."

Fiona shuddered. "Staff? I'm not sure if that's worse. Penelope from the grammar school got married in the summer, and she has become *very* lazy now that she has servants. I was horrified when I went to have tea with her last month. I don't think she does a thing for herself. I won't be like that. I'd hate that."

"I'm glad," her mother said, giving her arm a squeeze. "Stay exactly as you are, my darling. That is the only way you will be truly hap—"

Her words were severed by the sudden scream of "Thief! Thief! Stop that man!" that went up from the crowd that swarmed along Princes Street, somewhere up ahead.

A body bashed and weaved and feinted through the throng, clutching something close to his chest, his face half-covered by the shadow of a hood. He was running fast, seemingly oblivious, or uncaring, of those around him... and he was heading straight for Fiona. Panicked, she tried to step to the side, but her mother was trying to pull her to safety in the opposite direction.

In that moment of indecision, the man barrelled into Fiona's unguarded side, knocking into her so hard that she went flying. Her arm slipped out of her mother's and she tumbled to the ground, hitting her back against the flagstones with a wheezing, winding smack.

"Sorry," a voice growled, a rough hand seizing hold of her forearm, yanking her to her feet. "I didnae see ye there."

Startled, she peered up into the eyes of the hooded man, his hand still wrapped rightly around her forearm. His palm was coarse and calloused, his grip strong. And though he had just knocked her flat, there was a half-smile upon his lips, a flash of recognition passing across eyes the colour of a summer sky. Piercing blue.

She blinked at him, seeing something familiar in his face, something like a dream that would not quite cross the divide of sleep and awakening.

Those eyes... I know those eyes. She was certain of it, but before she could say a word or think of where she had seen him before, he darted off, pursued by two burly policemen in blue cloaks, blowing their whistles so loudly that the sound rattled in Fiona's skull for a few minutes afterwards.

"Are you hurt?" Beryl grasped her daughter by the arms, searching for any sign of injury.

Fiona shook her head slowly. "I'll live."

"Are you certain?"

Fiona nodded. "I'll have a bruise or two, but nothing I can't endure." She paused, thinking of her Bertha gown. "I hope they'll be gone by next week."

"Well, what a brute," her mother grumbled. "Are you sure you're not hurt?"

Fiona smiled stiffly, her back pinching. "I'm fine, which is more than can be said for that poor woman over there."

Surrounded by a small crowd, a wealthy woman in expensive bombazine, her neck adorned with fine jewels, was wailing inconsolably, clinging to a blue-cloaked constable as she cried, "My reticule! I had my favourite snuff box in there! Solid gold! Someone must catch that wretch!"

It shouldn't have been taken, but it's not as though you can't afford a new one. It's not as if someone died, Fiona wanted to say, but held her tongue. Her opinions of sharing wealth were not shared amongst high society, who considered every impoverished person to be the same: a horde of thugs and thieves and scoundrels who deserved their poverty.

"Let's eat those chestnuts at home," Beryl said, with a knowing smile. "We could give some to your father on the way."

Fiona nodded. "That sounds perfect to me."

But as they wandered to the chestnut stand, purchasing a brown paper bag of hot, sweet delights, and crossed to the other side of the street to make their way to the clockmaker's shop, Fiona's mind was elsewhere, fixed upon those two piercing blue eyes.

It was on the tip of her tongue, the precipice of her memory, but she could coax it no further.

I know him. He knew me. But how? She strained her brain fruitlessly, huffing through a mouthful of baking hot chestnut.

Indeed, it was only when they stepped into the clockmaker's shop, a bell ringing above the door to accompany the ticking of watches and clocks, that the stranger's face narrowed into perfect clarity.

She remembered where she knew him from, though four years had changed him, aged him, hardened his once-soft features from boyhood into manhood. But the eyes had not changed, aside from the fact that one had not been swollen with bruising.

Alastair... Her heart leapt and sank all at once, realising she was right. That thief was the boy from four winters ago. The boy who had saved her, helped her, and then disappeared into the dawn, leaving no trace. And though her life had not changed much, it appeared that his had taken a turn for the worst.

Chapter Seven

Christmas Eve arrived as it always did, with that shiver of excitement and trepidation. Fiona and her father had bid farewell to Beryl, after a cheery supper of leftovers from the feast they had shared on the 21st, and they were in fine spirits as they made the customary journey across the darkened park to the Old Town.

In her somewhat wiser, older years, Fiona had since learned why the drunkards had not moved from the benches when she was twelve-years-old, and always brought a few blankets with her. She left them where they could easily be taken by those who needed them, though she knew it would never be enough to stop people from falling asleep in the cold and never waking up again.

Her legs burned as she climbed up the slope to the Old Town, following the usual curving paths of slick cobblestones to Cockburn Street. Almost at the top, they paused and searched the surrounding area for any sign of miscreants, before slipping down the passageway of Jackson's Close, where the workshop awaited.

Tommy was already there, basking in the warm glow of a new woodstove that *almost* took the chill from the room. A kettle steamed on top of the stove, and three cups were ready to be filled with hot tea to bolster their strength for the evening to come.

"What time d'ye call this?" Tommy grinned, pouring out the tea. "I was worried ye'd got so high-and-mighty that ye were nae comin'."

Fiona cast him a mock withering look. "I'm not getting high-and-mighty. Pa would never allow it." She walked to Tommy and gave him a hug, his huge bear-like arms squeezing her so tight she feared for her ribs. "In fact, my mama said I might have staff to tend to me if I marry this Kelvin boy, and I was appalled. I don't want staff. What would I do with staff?"

"Our wee lass is all grown up." Tommy pretended to wipe a tear from his cheek, as Donal laughed.

"Daenae say that. I'm strugglin' with all this betrothal nonsense enough as it is," her father said, pulling a face. "Seems like yesterday she was sittin' on me shoulders, beggin' to feed the ducks."

Tommy shrugged. "I wouldnae mind takin' her place, though yer shoulders might nae be able to bear it."

"Nothing is confirmed yet," Fiona reminded them. "It's just a meeting with him and his family. But if he keeps me from spending Christmas Eve with the two of you, he can forget it."

Tommy chuckled. "That's the Fiona I ken. Tough as old leather, like yer da."

"Are we quite finished discussing my future?" she said with a smile. "We've got sacks to fill and deliveries to make, and the longer we spend chatting, the longer those fine people are going to have to wait for the toys. Come on, let's drink this tea and set to work! Chop-chop!"

Feigning a grumble, Tommy and Donal obeyed, taking their tea to the workbench as the usual preparations began. Donal took down the toys, Fiona wrapped, and Tommy put the goods carefully in the waiting sacks. They had become quicker over the past four years, in every respect, turning the stocking of the sacks into a fine art.

Before long, they were done, stuffed sacks lined up against the far wall. Taking one apiece, the trio headed back out of the workshop and into the surprisingly mild night. Snow had fallen here and there for the past few days, but none had stuck, and though Fiona dearly loved the snow, she was glad it was not so cold, not for her sake but for the sake of those who had no home to return to.

"Good luck," her father said as they reached the stretch of the Royal Mile. He bent and kissed her brow. "Keep yer wits about ye, and I'll see ye for breakfast at dawn, if nae before."

Fiona kissed her father's cheek in return. "The same goes for you, Papa. If you see trouble, you run, and you don't stop until you're safe."

"Daenae let nothin' happen to me wee ducklin', Tommy," her father said, his tone light, his expression serious. "Ye ken I'm only trustin' ye with her care because ye're twice the size of me."

Tommy chuckled, resting a hand on Fiona's shoulder. "She'll be safe with me, same as always."

"Aye, well…" Donal smiled, and, with a nod of his head, he began walking northwards up the Royal Mile, whilst Fiona and Tommy turned southwards. It was something they had trialled two years prior, in order to cover more ground, more quickly, and though Fiona worried for her father all night, and he undoubtedly worried for her, it worked perfectly.

"So, ye're getting' married, eh?" Tommy asked.

Fiona shrugged. "It's what's expected. I'm six-and-ten now, and the McKintosh family are a good family. That's what everyone keeps saying—they're a "good family." Not sure I know what that means, but plenty of my friends are already married, so I suppose it's what I should do too. How's your wife?"

"Ruin' the day she married me," Tommy replied, laughing. "She's askin' when ye're goin' to come for tea again. The bairns, too. They adore ye."

Fiona pulled an apologetic face. "I'll try to come soon. New Year's Day, perhaps?"

"They'd like that."

They'd just cut down Blackfriars Street, where they often started their work, when something caught Fiona's eye. Or, rather, the noise caught her attention. In the middle of the street, three figures seemed to be in the midst of a scrap. Two wore the telltale blue cloaks of the constabulary, whilst the third was dressed all in black, one of the constables holding onto the man in black's collar as if his life depended on it.

"I've nae done anythin'!" the captured man barked. "I was on me way home!"

"Aye, with a bag full of stolen goods!" one of the constables shouted back.

Fiona noticed the hessian sack clutched in the captive's hand, which the second constable was trying to pull loose. But it was *that* voice that made her halt sharply. It had deepened, but she would have known it anywhere. She had dreamed of it often enough in the past four years, wondering what had become of the boy who had so desperately wanted to give toys to the people of the Old Town.

She knew she should not involve herself, knew she should keep well away, but before she could stop herself, she was striding forward, hurrying toward the scuffle.

"Excuse me, sirs. What are you doing to my friend?" she demanded to know, her heart thudding violently in her chest as Alastair's blue eyes squinted at her, confused.

The constables stared at her as if she had escaped from an asylum.

"*This* is a friend of yers?" one asked, eyeing her from her shiny shoes to her fur trimmed coat.

Fiona nodded. "He's employed by my father." She gestured to Tommy, who had walked up behind her, hoping he would play along. "We deliver gifts to the children of the Old Town on Christmas Eve. I think we might have met you before—last year. The constabulary knows about us, so I'm sure you've been told to look out for us."

The constables exchanged a look, but they did not loosen their grip on Alastair.

"This man is a thief, miss," one said. "Might be ye've mistaken him for someone else. He's got stolen goods in that sack."

Fiona shook her head effusively. "No, he has toys." She opened up her own sack to show them the contents. "My father here makes them, and then we give them to the needy. My friend began earlier than my father and I, but I promise he has toys in that sack. That's why he's holding on so tight, because they're precious, and if you think he's a thief, he was probably worried you'd try to take them."

"Aye, she's tellin' the truth," Tommy came in confidently. "I've kenned this lad for years. Used to be trouble, aye, but he's changed his ways 'cause he has employment now. Ye ken what it's like."

The constables blinked up at Tommy, towering over them with arms as thick as their heads, and quickly glanced at one another, as if deciding whether or not it was worth quarrelling with such a huge bear of a man. They seemed to choose the easy path, one constable letting go of Alastair's collar as the other released his grip on the sack of miscellaneous goods.

"So, ye're the toy man we've heard so much about?" The first constable hesitated. "I daenae suppose ye've a dolly in there, do ye?"

Tommy dipped into his sack. "What colour hair do ye want?"

"As close to blonde as ye've got?" The constable smiled nervously, stretching out his hand.

Finding a yellow-haired doll, Tommy passed it over, smiling at the second constable. "Anythin' for ye?"

"One of those frogs that make a sound?"

Tommy nodded and reached into Fiona's sack for a wooden frog with a ridged back, that sort of croaked when you ran a little stick across it. "A frog for ye, a dolly for ye. Now, can we carry on with what we're doin'? We've a lot of people to visit, and nae very long to do it."

"Aye, be on yer way," the constable with the frog said, shooting a glare at Alastair. "And stay together, if ye've any sense. We daenae want any more trouble from ye."

Alastair flung his sack over his shoulder. "I'll be good as anythin', sir. All I want to do is bring a smile to the faces of those who havenae got too much to smile about. Daenae ye worry about me."

The constable narrowed his eyes but, with a nod to Tommy and Fiona, he went on his way with his associate, the two men wandering past the trio and vanishing around the corner, onto the Royal Mile.

The moment they were gone, Fiona lunged for Alastair's hessian sack, swiping it from his shoulder before he realised what she was doing. He tried to grab it back, but he was a second too slow. She whirled away from him and, with Tommy stepping between them, keeping Alastair at arm's length, she opened the bag and peered inside. Silver and silk winked back at her: handkerchiefs, cutlery, candlesticks, alongside a thick woollen coat, several reticules, and some leather wallets.

"You can have this," Fiona said, pulling out the coat and throwing it at Alastair. "The rest is confiscated and will be returned if it can be. You can tell me where you stole it from and I'll take it back, making up a story about finding the bag if I have to. But, right now, you're delaying us, and I know that's not something you want to do, not if you're anything like the boy I remember from four years ago. Then again, it does seem like a lot has changed."

She heard him splutter, trying to form the words to protest, but she had already wandered off down Blackfriars Street to begin the only task that mattered. But as she walked, she heard Tommy explode into laughter, the warm, rumbling sound bringing a pleased smile to her face. And looking back, she saw Alastair trailing miserably at Tommy's side, dragging his feet but joining the group nonetheless.

You're not running off this time, Alastair, she vowed. After all, she still owed him a gift.

Chapter Eight

Within an hour of beginning the deliveries, greeting the mothers and fathers who had been waiting, exchanging stories of how their lives had been since last meeting, sharing a tipple and a few morsels of food with those who had were keen to share, Fiona glimpsed something of the boy that she remembered in the young man that Alastair had become.

"Ye were here four years back, were ye nae?" a sharp-eyed woman said to him, grabbing him by the hand and pulling him into a hug he could not escape. "I remember worryin' for the fate of ye! Ye were bare as a babe, yer lips all blue. Warms me heart to see ye've become a strappin' lad."

Fiona smiled at the scene. "I couldn't have done any of it without him, Mrs. Donohue."

"Och, ye were such a sweet pair. So earnest, and in that snowstorm too!" Mrs. Donohue said, releasing Alastair just enough to take a good look at him. "We were mighty grateful for ye, I'll tell ye that, with yer da bein' poorly an' all. Now, I look forward to *ye* comin' here of a Christmas Eve. Miss Christmas herself with her beardy Christmas bear followin' her round."

Tommy laughed his best belly laugh. "Who needs reindeer, eh?"

"At least ye're wearin' proper clothes this time," Mrs. Donohue said to Alastair, making her final observation of him. "Speakin' of reindeer, that coat looks dear. Warm, I'll bet. Ye must've done well for yerself."

Alastair lowered his gaze, scuffing his toe against a small pile of slush. "Aye, I've nae done so bad."

"I imagine ye've had to work hard to win the heart of Miss Christmas," Mrs. Donohue teased. "She speaks nice and dresses nice, so she'd nae settle for any ruffian, eh?"

Alastair's cheeks bloomed pink. "I wouldnae ken, Ma'am. She's me... old friend, is all."

"Och, ye cannae kid a kidder," Mrs. Donohue laughed. "I seen ye glancin' all shy at each other four years back. Daenae imagine aught has changed, considerin' how beautiful she is, and how fancy ye're dressin' now. Might be a new Mr and Mrs. Christmas this time next year, eh?"

Alastair stepped back. "Ye should pick a gift, Ma'am. We've other homes to get to."

"I've embarrassed the lad." Mrs. Donohue looked delighted with herself as she chose two toys from the sack for boys. "But I'll be sayin' "I told ye so" when ye come back next year, I'd stake me stash of coal on it."

As they bid farewell to Mrs. Donohue and moved on to the next door, Alastair became sullen again, refusing to look at

Fiona. And though Tommy was usually the first to leap on a jest, he did not make any jokes at the younger man's expense as they continued into the dark, as though he knew it was not appropriate, even for him.

But, gradually, as the hours passed and the sacks emptied, Alastair's mood improved, his eyes brightening, his face cracking into ready smiles, his eagerness showing in the stories he told and the stories he asked for, as he invited the people of the Old Town to take their pick of Donal's masterpieces.

It was as if he had finally taken off a coat of a different kind, a coat of bitterness and anger, letting it fall from his shoulders as he involved himself in the festive spirit of the night.

"If they give me another bite to eat, I'll be sick," he complained, as the trio made their first journey back to the workshop to gather more toys. "They shouldnae do it, ye ken, but they do. It'll never nae amaze me. Of course, it's different if ye're on the corner of the street with yer hands out, beggin'— then, no one gives ye so much as a morsel."

Fiona cast him a sideways glance. "Has that happened to you?"

"A few times," he replied, stuffing his hands deep into the pockets of the stolen coat. It suited him, making him appear almost like a gentleman. "Nae for a while, though."

Indeed, he had become rather handsome in the years that had passed. His face and body had filled out, he had shot up like a weed, and even with the coat hiding his physique, he had the build of someone who could protect themselves and others.

His features had strengthened too, his jaw strong, his cheekbones defined, his beautiful eyes warm when they wanted to be. Fiona was just glad that he no longer looked like he was starving, but she feared what he had endured since he disappeared into the night on that strange Christmas Eve.

"Is that why you turned to stealing?" Fiona swallowed thickly, her stomach fluttering with nerves. She knew better than to ask for someone's story if they were not willing to tell it, but part of her simply had to know: the part of her that had thought of him often, fearing the worst.

Alastair sniffed. "I daenae think of it is as stealin' if it's taken from someone who doesnae need it, and can afford to replace it," he said, tilting his chin up defiantly. "But me—I need them things. I need them to keep me warm, to keep a roof over me head, to keep me fed."

"I'm not giving them back," Fiona insisted, the faint jangle of the thieved goods taunting.

He narrowed his eyes at her. "Then, I'll take the value of what *ye've* stolen from me from yer da's workshop." He lowered his voice so that Tommy would not overhear. "I remember where it is. Even if I didnae, ye're leadin' me right there."

"I don't believe you," she said, hoping she did not sound as doubtful as she felt. "I know what this means to you, Alastair. Besides, if you meant to do something like that, you would have done it already. You would have done it long before I first met you, when you were struggling far more than I think you are now."

He rolled his eyes. "Aye, well, maybe I'm nae low enough to steal toys from bairns, but I will have me bag back by the time the sun rises. It's nae yers to keep and I'm nae goin' to tell ye where I stole the things from, so ye willnae be able to give any of it back."

"Why steal it in the first place?" Fiona paused. "I'm not judging you, I'm genuinely curious. I've… often wondered what became of you after you left that night. For a while, I wasn't even sure you existed. I took ill with a fever after that Christmas Eve, you see, and… I thought the fever had conjured you, so I would have the strength to finish my father's work."

His expression softened, his eyes widening slightly. "Ye got sick?"

"I recovered."

"Aye, well, ye wouldnae be here if ye hadnae." He laughed softly. "I'm sorry ye got sick. I'm sorry I ran off like that too, nae because I didnae say farewell or anythin', but because I didnae get me gift."

Fiona smiled. "You were good at skirting around hard questions back then, too."

"I'm a thief," he said with a smirk. "I'm good at skirtin' around most things. Anyway, ye wouldnae understand. Ye help yer da, and that's not a thing to sniff at, but ye're still from the other side of the park."

Fiona straightened up. "So, allow me to understand. Enlighten me. Maybe, I can help you, too." She hesitated. "How about this—if you tell me, I'll let you have *one* of the things you stole."

"Ye'll have to give me all of it," he replied, his eyes turning flinty once more. "If ye daenae, ye willnae find me here next year. Ye willnae find me here come New Year, either. I'll have me throat slit and me body thrown into a bog outside the city, and nay one will ever ken what happened to me."

Fiona halted sharply, a gasp raking out of her throat. "What?"

"Ye said ye wanted to ken why I thieve. Have ye changed yer mind?"

She shook her head slowly, uncertainly.

"I'm in some trouble," he explained, burrowing his chin into the collar of the woollen coat. "I need to sell what's in that sack of things I stole, else I willnae be able to get *out* of the trouble I'm in. And that's when—" He lifted his head and traced a fingertip across his throat. "But ye be righteous if ye like. Ye defend the folk who willnae miss what I took, if that makes ye feel better. Still, ye should ken that if ye daenae give it back, ye'll be sealin' me fate."

Fiona's gaze flitted desperately toward Tommy, who had approached to see why the pair had stopped in the middle of the icy street. He cast Fiona a fond smile and shrugged, as if to say, *"He's got a point."*

"Tommy?" she pressed, needing his advice.

Tommy shrugged again. "It's nae business of mine, but if it were me, I would think to meself... it's Christmas. Why nae give a poor man a gift?"

Fiona chewed her lower lip, thinking hard.

Her mind drifted back to the weeping woman on Princes Street, wailing about her lost, solid gold snuff box as if it were a legitimate tragedy. A moment later, she pictured the people of the Old Town, living in rot and destitution, doing their best to survive and to feed their hungry children.

She thought of the haunted eyes of mothers, selecting one less gift from the sack that year. She thought of the food and drink that those people shared with her, though she wore new shoes and an expensive coat.

"I need you to make me a promise," Fiona murmured, meeting Alastair's anxious gaze.

He frowned. "What sort of promise?"

"I need you to swear that you won't let anyone slit your throat and throw you in a bog, if I give this sack back to you."

He smiled, his entire face brightening. "I swear it to ye."

"Very well, then... sell everything for the highest price you can get and get yourself out of trouble." She plucked the bag of stolen goods out of the empty sack that had held toys and passed it to Alastair. "There's a solid gold snuff box in that reticule you stole a few days ago, if you hadn't found it yet."

He blinked in surprise. "I didnae think ye recognised me." He paused, a little sheepish. "How's yer back? I really didnae mean to knock into ye like that. It's nae me intention to hurt anyone."

"My back is fine," she replied stiffly. "A few bruises, but nothing to complain about."

He dropped his chin to his chest. "Still, I'm sorry."

"You're forgiven."

Tommy cleared his throat. "And we've got work to do, so if ye're finished chatterin' like monkeys, we ought to press on."

"I'll say me farewells here and leave ye to it," Alastair said abruptly, and Fiona's heart lurched into her throat, her hand shooting out to grab his wrist without thinking.

"You can't," she urged.

Alastair arched an eyebrow. "Why can I nae?"

"Because… because you must be frozen!" she blurted out. "You should come to the workshop and have something warm to drink, at the very least, and then you can go on your merry way. And if you should decide that you might like to keep helping us tonight, then… we'd be happy to have you."

Tommy grinned, folding his arms across his barrel chest as he watched Fiona squirming, clearly amused by what he was seeing. Fiona, meanwhile, did not see what was so funny about it.

She merely wanted to pay Alastair back for the help he had given her four years ago, that was all. At least, that was what she was determined to convince herself was true.

Alastair slung the sack of stolen goods over his shoulder and chinned up the street. "I willnae say nay to somethin' warm to drink, but I'll nae be stayin' to help for the rest of the night. I've got work of me own to do."

"As you prefer," Fiona said thickly, leading the way back to the workshop.

***

Fiona entered the workshop first, rushing to the woodstove to put fresh water into the kettle, from the bucket beside the stove. She almost did not dare to look back as she busied herself, but as a few minutes went by, and she heard no sound, curiosity prompted her to turn around to see where everyone was.

Tommy leaned against the doorjamb, watching with a sad expression that Fiona could not read. Meanwhile, Alastair stood by the workbench, running his fingertips along the tools and dried-up splashes of paint, touching the old grooves from long ago mistakes.

And when he came across a half-finished nutcracker, he cradled it gently in his hands, turning it over, lifting it to the hazy light of a lantern to see it in closer detail. His eyes gleamed wetly, his mouth pressed in a tight line that trembled just a little.

"A long time ago, this used to be me da's workshop," he said quietly, as if to himself. "I'd forgotten how… beautiful it is. How much I missed it."

Chapter Nine

"I've been afraid of knockin' on this door for years," Alastair continued, still admiring the nutcracker in his hand. "I kenned there was another toymaker here, and that he was deliverin' toys to all the children of the Old Town, and I desperately wanted to help… but I couldnae bring meself to knock on this door. And when ye were about to invite me in, Miss Fiona, I… couldnae do it. I ran. I couldnae… face it."

Fiona stared at him, not daring to move or say a word in case it made him stop. But Tommy seemed to know how to keep the story going, as he asked, "Yer father was a toymaker, too?"

"Aye," Alastair said softly. "Made the most… perfect wooden toys ye could imagine. He could make whatever anyone asked for. If they came in wantin' a toy badger, he could do it, and it'd look just like what it was meant to be. At our lodgings, we had shelves upon shelves of his creations, and though me ma would complain when he brought another one home that he thought we might like, she'd always put it up on a shelf and smile at it.

"He wasnae as famous as yer da, Miss Fiona, but he was famous enough," he carried on thickly. "I think he might've been more famous, if he'd had the chance. There were some fine folk comin' to his workshop to ask for toys, and he was thinkin' of rentin' a shop nae far from here, so he could sell his wares. It was a long time ago, but… I remember him havin' a meetin' arranged to sign the contracts for a shop. He was… excited about it. Bought us cakes and mince pies to celebrate. Miss Fiona, do ye remember I told ye about me very best Christmas Eve?"

Fiona nodded, her heart in her throat. "I do. You said it was an ordinary Christmas Eve. You had your first mince pie, and you sat around the fireplace with your mother and father, singing carols. There was a tree made of twigs, and you'd made something for your mother."

"I wanted to be like me da," Alastair explained with a sad smile. "It was me first attempt at whittlin'. I made me ma a hedgehog, 'cause they were her favourites. It wasnae a very pretty hedgehog, but ye could mostly tell what it was. And I was desperate to give it to her, but she said I had to wait 'til Christmas mornin'. We ate the cakes, da let me have a nip of whisky, and then me ma put me to bed. I didnae even hear them leave the lodgings that night. Probably 'cause of the whisky."

Tommy cleared his throat, as if dislodging a lump. "What happened?"

"They went down the street to a hootenanny that me ma's friend, Mrs. Finch, was havin' for Christmas Eve. They did it every year and I was always furious that they wouldnae let me go with them, but I was too excited about wakin' up to give me ma her hedgehog that I daenae think I even thought about it that night." Alastair swallowed loudly. "Maybe, me da gave me more than a nip, mixed in with a cup of milk, 'cause I slept like the dead. When I finally woke up, I could hear a cock crowin' from the yard below. It was dark out and the fire had died, but I figured it must've been gettin' close to dawn.

"I clambered out of bed and went behind this… partition we had in the main room, for me ma and da. They were nae there. The cot was made, hadnae been slept in." A tear escaped his eye, trailing down his swarthy cheek. "I remembered they must've gone to Mrs. Finch's, so I put on some tea and stoked the fire, waitin' for them to come back. Sometimes, if the hootenanny was good, they wouldnae return 'til late, so… I just sat there and waited, holdin' that stupid hedgehog in me hands."

Tommy touched a hooked finger to his cheek, discreetly brushing something away. "They didnae come back?"

"Nay, they didnae," Alastair replied, setting the nutcracker down. "I waited 'til noon, then I put on me da's old cloak and went in search of them. Mrs. Finch's wasnae too far. Just the top end of the same street. The smell hit me first." He banged on his chest, choking as if he could smell it anew. "Smoke. Nae the wood kind, but the burnin' kind. I daenae ken if that makes sense, but… it's a bitter smell. Sticks in yer throat, makes yer eyes water.

"There were folk cryin' in the street. Screamin', like." Alastair shook his head. "It had rained, so the blaze didnae spread so far, but it had gutted the whole tenement where Mrs. Finch lived. I couldnae tell ye, even now, how many people died that day. See, it started at the ground floor, eating up the stairwells, trappin' everyone above inside. Nay one could get out." He took a shaky breath. "Me ma and da were halfway up. I buried them a few days after Christmas, along with the rest, and though I sold every last toy me da had to survive, I kept that bloody hedgehog."

He drew a misshapen chunk of wood out of his pocket and set it on the workbench beside the nutcracker. Jagged spikes had been worn smooth, a narrow snout close to breaking off, the rounded shape lopsided. Yet, though crude, Fiona could see the hedgehog it was supposed to be.

"I've been on me own ever since," Alastair murmured, gently stroking the spikes of the hedgehog. "But, the followin' year, the queerest thing happened. There were lights on in the workshop again. I heard the sounds of someone makin' toys again. And I watched a man creepin' out on Christmas Eve with a sack slung over his shoulder. Then, on Christmas mornin', I watched the other bairns rushin' out into the streets to show their friends the new toys that had appeared in the night. It was like magic. Yet, nay toy had come to me. The year after, I watched and waited, wonderin' if, that year, a toy would find its way to me. I wanted to knock and ask for one, but... like I said, I could never muster the courage. I've nae been in this workshop since I was six. Eleven years, and here I am. It hasnae changed a bit."

For a long while, no one said another word. Tommy finished the job of pouring out cups of tea, while Alastair sat on the stool by the workbench, the hedgehog clenched in his hand.

Fiona, on the other hand, stood frozen by the woodstove, her heart broken by Alastair's story.

Yet, it cracked further, contemplating all of the things he had left out, all of the gaps in between that he had not elaborated upon. What had a six-year-old boy had to suffer in order to survive?

How many bitterly cold nights had he spent on the street? How many times had he had a brush with death?

How had he endured? She knew she would not have been able to, had she been in his position. And there she was, trying to deny him a sack of stolen goods that would not be missed by anyone.

At length, she got her legs to work again, and went to the stuffed sacks that still lined the wall, waiting to be delivered, and carried one to him. "Would you like a toy now? I do still owe you one from four years ago." She gestured to the bookcases. "Or, you could have one of my father's clockwork ones. You... deserve one."

Alastair shook his head, his cheeks turning red. "I'm too old for toys." He hesitated, taking a sip of his tea to wet his throat. "But... I would like to continue to help ye tonight, if ye'll still have me? Ye see, I might nae have got a toy, but those gifts cheered the hearts of a thousand bairns like me. Seein' yer da take them all around the Old Town; I think it reminded me that there's good in the world, ye ken? I wouldnae mind bein' part of that good again."

"We'd be glad to have ye," Tommy interjected, pausing to ruffle Fiona's hair.

She glared at him. "What did you do that for?"

"Thought I saw a spider," Tommy replied, flashing a grin as he fetched a sack for himself and a sack for Alastair.

A short while later, they were back in the biting cold, huddled together as they walked the streets of Edinburgh's Old Town. Yet, Alastair seemed lighter, his smile wide as he danced a jig or two, calling himself "Master Christmas" and laughing as if it was the greatest feeling in the world.

Fiona watched him, her own spirits rising, for though he looked like a man now, he had not lost too much the boy she remembered. He had merely been dormant for a while.

A sharp nudge to her arm jolted her out of her pleasant thoughts.

"Ye've got a rich boy waitin' for ye," Tommy teased, wiggling his eyebrows. "Ye shouldnae be gawpin' at that wee ruffian. Och, ye might be more like yer ma than I thought."

"I wasn't gawping at him," Fiona protested in a hushed whisper, jabbing Tommy in the ribs with her elbow. "I'm just... happy that he's happy."

Tommy chuckled. "Aye, of course that's all there is to it. That's why ye're starin' at him like ye're hopelessly in love."

"I am not!" She jabbed him harder in the ribs. "You're a wicked one, Tommy Mulhern. Next year, I'm going to insist on delivering the gifts with my father. He might not be as monstrous as you, but he doesn't delight in teasing me."

Tommy laughed. "Och, it must be serious, if ye're tellin' me off for teasin' ye instead of banterin' back."

"Oh... oh... hush!" she grumbled, striding ahead of him.

I do not have a fancy for Alastair, she fumed silently… even if he was handsome and charming and, once upon a winter's night, he had saved her life.

Chapter Ten

The next evening, full to the brim with a feast of cold cuts and buttery potatoes and the satisfaction of knowing that some lives were just a little bit merrier that day, Fiona strolled with her father to the workshop for the final part of their charitable exploits.

"We really ought to see if Alastair wants to help us next year," Fiona said with a fond smile, as she looped her arm through her father's. Hastily, she corrected herself. "Help you, I mean. I might not be able to escape for the night, and though it used to work with just two, I think three is better."

Donal squinted down at her daughter. "Ye've taken a shine to his lad, eh?"

"I'm... grateful to him," she replied. "You ought to be too."

Her father smiled. "I am, me wee ducklin'. Though, I'll be honest, I never thought he actually existed. I wish he would've stayed to meet me. I mean, I ken I *should* believe what ye and Tommy told me, but ye might be playin' a trick on me."

"He does exist, Papa. I told him that he should meet us at the workshop tonight, to help take everything to the church, so perhaps you *will* be able to confirm that he's real," she said in earnest, hoping beyond hope that Alastair would be there when they turned into the passageway of Jackson's Close. "As if we would play such an elaborate trick on you."

Donal chuckled. "Tommy would, but ye wouldnae—ye're right about that."

Taking one or two sacks of gifts was something they had begun to do the year after Fiona's first outing. She had seeded the idea after seeing where Alastair had been living.

"What about those who don't have a home?" she remembered asking, as she had sat coughing by the woodstove, watching her father wash away the blood on Tommy's battered face. *"Is there a way we can deliver toys to them? We could search every alleyway, I suppose, but… there must be a better way."*

Tommy, in a croaky voice, had replied, *"The church. Give some toys to the church."*

Indeed, Fiona now wondered if that was why Alastair's story had made her heart ache so much, for now they had a way to get toys to the children who were living on the streets, whilst he had been left without. Waiting endlessly, trying to gather the courage to knock on the workshop door.

"I think he has a good heart," Fiona said, more to herself than to her father, as they groaned their way up the familiar slope of Cockburn Street.

Upon opening the workshop door, all of Fiona's merriment evaporated like a puff of winter breath on the wind. Tommy sat by the woodstove with his head in his hands, surrounded by chaos. Bookcases had been torn down, shelves ripped from the walls, floorboards pried up, the workbench drawers strewn across the ground, all of the tools and gifts that had been left the previous night, gone.

It was all gone, even the clockwork masterpieces that had been on those shelves for at least four years; the detailed creations that her father had never been able to give away, claiming he was saving them for his grandchildren.

"They must've come after we left this mornin'," Tommy said, his voice thick with misery. His eyes were rimmed with red, as if he had been crying. "I was certain I couldnae see anyone watchin'. I locked the door. We were… so careful. I mean, it's been four years since we were threatened, and nothin' has gone missin'."

"Do you think it was those men?" Fiona choked out, aghast at the scene before her, like someone had stolen the magic from every corner of the workshop, leaving it bland and dull and sad to behold.

Tommy shrugged. "I daenae ken." His expression. "Nay, I wouldnae like to say."

"What do you mean?" Fiona peered at him, an uneasy feeling beginning to squirm in her chest, vermicular.

Tommy wiped his nose on the back of his sleeve. "Nothin'. It doesnae matter."

But she knew what he meant. She knew why he did not want to say it out loud, yet they were both thinking it.

The only difference between the last few years and last night was Alastair. Alastair who had admitted he was in trouble and needed enough money to get himself *out* of trouble.

What if the contents of the sack had not been enough? What if he had needed more, and quickly?

What if, in his desperation, he had led those he owed a debt to, to the workshop? The wooden toys might not have been worth much, but the clockwork toys would have been worth a small fortune.

No, he wouldn't do that, she scolded herself, remembering his story, and the glee upon his face when he had delivered the gifts with her and Tommy.

Even if he was desperate, he would not have revealed the location of the workshop. He would not have offered up gifts intended for needy children, just to save his own skin... would he?

"I have more!" her father said suddenly, clapping his hands together. "This is... unfortunate, aye, but I have more."

Tommy raised an eyebrow. "Where? If ye hid some away under the floorboards, they're nae there anymore."

"I have half a sack's worth, perhaps, hidden at the back of the clock shop," Donal replied at a clip, as though speaking his thoughts as they popped into his head. "I have some more at the apartments. I reckon we can fill at least one sack, aye. It's nae as much as I'd like, but it's somethin'. And I promised the church. We've got to give 'em somethin'."

Tommy nodded, straightening up. "Aye, we do." He paused. "But ye cannae make yer toys here any more. After today, ye find someplace else to make 'em. I always said this wasnae safe, but... I'll hang the scoundrels if I get me hands on 'em."

"One thing at a time," Donal told him, taking a breath. "Fiona, ye wait at Greyfriars and let 'em ken we're comin'. Tommy, ye come with me to the shop. I cannae say for certain how many toys I have hidden, so if there's more than I reckon, I'll need yer strength."

Tommy pursed his lips. "Ye cannae send the lass off to Greyfriars on her own."

"He can," Fiona insisted. "I know the way. I'll go straight there, and I won't move until you two arrive. I'll be well enough once I'm inside the church."

Donal puffed out a strained breath. "We daenae have a choice, Tommy. I need ye, and I'm the only one with a key. It has to be us." He looked to Fiona. "Promise ye'll go straight there, and ye'll keep yer wits about ye."

"I promise," Fiona vowed, swallowing the tremor of trepidation that threatened to shake her voice. She had never wandered the Old Town alone, much less at night, but she wanted to prove to her father that she could be brave. "There are bairns who'll be hoping for a gift. I'm not going to be the one to disappoint them."

Tommy shook his head, steadfast. "Ye go to the shop, Donal. I'll take Fiona to the kirk, then I'll come to ye. I'm nae lettin' her walk alone tonight, nae after this has happened. Ye daenae ken if *someone* might still be watchin' and waitin'."

Fiona could not ignore the emphasis. She knew precisely who Tommy was worried about, and though she did not share in his concerns, she would not waste time arguing. "Let's hurry, then. After all, Tommy, you're not built for running. It'll take you longer than you think to get to my pa and the shop."

"The gall of ye," Tommy retorted, but the hint of a smile tugged at his lips, restoring her faith that all might yet be well.

***

Fiona did not know how long she had been waiting, but it felt like an eternity. The clergymen had invited her into the church, but it had been colder inside than outside, and the two clergymen had eyed her strangely, prompting her to insist on keeping her vigil out in the kirkyard itself.

She sat on the front steps of the church, watching a small terrier who seemed to have made a bed of one of the graves. He lay flat, his chin resting on his paws, peering right back at her. She seemed to remember him being called "Bobby," the loyal companion to a man who had died a few years prior.

"Bobby," she called, whistling softly. "Bobby, come here."

The terrier closed his eyes, ignoring her. Evidently, she was disturbing his slumber, though his very presence there made her feel less afraid of the kirkyard. It was a sorrowful place, even in daylight, but in the darkness, with fog rolling in, it was the very last place she would have chosen to be.

He'd bark if there was anything to be scared of, she told herself, somewhat enamoured with the small terrier, who had remained so heartbreakingly loyal, never leaving his owner's side even though death had parted them.

She had often wanted a dog to keep her company, but her mother and father had refused.

Just then, the dog raised his head, his keen eyes peering at something off to the left of Fiona. She followed his line of sight, her heart seizing in her chest as she saw what he was looking at. A pale face peered out from behind a tree, ghostly in the foggy moonlight. He could not have been older than six or seven, his clothes so frayed and ragged that he might as well have been wearing nothing at all.

The dog settled back down, reassuring Fiona that she was not, in fact, seeing a ghost. Not one with ill intentions, anyway.

Suddenly, the boy met her gaze, a harsh gasp cutting through the air, before he turned and ran.

Before she knew it, she was taking off after him, thinking of Alastair and the boy he had been, long before she had met him. Perhaps, if someone had offered *him* some kindness, he might not have felt like he was so desperately alone. And though she had no toys to offer, she *did* have money in her coin purse and the coat off her back to keep him from freezing to death.

"You! Halt!" she called out as she ran, stumbling across gnarled tree roots and the fallen headstones of forgotten men and women.

The boy stayed just ahead of her, darting this way and that, leading her into the deepest, darkest reaches of the kirkyard, past elms and oaks and yew trees, and around eerie iron mortsafes—caged graves, designed to keep out the resurrectionists she had heard terrible things about. Tales from the girls at her old grammar school, though how much those girls could be believed, she was not sure.

But as the darkness swept in like a vast cloak, the light from the church too far away to offer any guidance, and with the fog growing thicker around her, she soon lost sight of the boy all together.

"I mean you no harm!" she whispered, the skin prickling at the nape of her neck, a cold sweat following the line of her spine. "I want to give you some money. You could come into the church with me and wait for a gift, if you like?"

No one answered, the fog muffling the sound of the world beyond the walls of the kirkyard, until she wondered if she had stepped into another realm entirely: the land of the dead, where ghosts wandered at their leisure, and might take joy in frightening her.

"Boy?" she hissed, hugging herself. "Could you come out, please? I really don't mean you any harm."

She squinted into the fog as if that might help her to hear better, her heart pounding hard in her chest. At that moment, a noise drifted dully toward her. A sawing, soughing sound, coming from somewhere up ahead.

Clasping a hand to her chest to try and slow her frantic breaths, she crept toward the thick trunk of a tree and slipped behind it, peering into the gloom, hoping to make out the person who was making that awful sawing sound.

She had learned from her years of charitable service to the Old Town that it was best not to be noticed, but she had to know if it was the boy. She did not know why she was so determined, when she had seen countless boys like him throughout the slums, yet she could not leave without ensuring he was well.

A gust of icy wind cajoled the fog, clearing a swathe of it for just a moment. And that moment was all she needed.

She clamped a hand over her mouth, stifling a gasp. A familiar figure stood at the edge of what appeared to be a fresh grave, a shovel sticking up beside a small mound of earth as he mopped his brow with a dirty handkerchief.

The girls were telling the truth, she realised in abject horror, remembering how they would whisper of the infamous body snatchers, Burke and Hare. Yet, Fiona had chosen to believe they were just made-up tales, intended to scare children and young women alike. She had not thought it possible that anyone could be wretched enough to dig up someone else's loved one for money.

But it was obvious what was happening, right in front of her. The tales were not pretend at all. And Alastair was the one with the shovel, driving it into the cold earth to bring up his rotting treasure, on Christmas Day of all days.

Chapter Eleven

"What in heaven's name do you think you're doing?" Fiona strode out to confront Alastair, forgetting about ghosts and ghouls. The only ghoul in that kirkyard was him, as far as she was concerned.

Alastair jumped violently, dropping his shovel. He whirled around, his face stricken as his crystalline blue eyes met hers, flinching slightly under the vehemence of her glare. She watched his throat bob as he slowly put up his hands in a gesture of surrender. "It's nae what it looks like," he fumbled to say.

"So, you're not robbing a grave?"

He gulped loudly. "Actually, nay. I'm nae robbin' it."

"You are taking the body from where it belongs," she hissed. "I'd call that thievery, wouldn't you?"

He licked his dry lips. "Aye, I suppose, but... I was takin' it to a couple of students from the university. I wasnae goin' to take anythin'. They offered good money for it."

"Him," Fiona snapped, her eyes skimming over the name on the headstone. "*He* was a him. He was a person, and you're... you're... desecrating his grave! Keep stealing from the rich if you need money, or—heaven forbid—ask for some help, but don't do... this, for goodness' sake!"

Alastair sank down to the ground, sitting right there in the dirt. "It wasnae enough. I couldnae sell half of what I stole, and I couldnae get a good price for what I could sell. I kenned this would be easy coin—a pal of mine told me about it. I needed the coin, and I needed it quickly, Fiona." He puffed a steamy breath into the frigid air. "Do ye think this is somethin' I want to be doin'? Do ye think this is what I thought I'd be doin' when I was a bairn? It's nae a choice, lass. It's... survivin' to see another day. I willnae even get a headstone when it's me turn, and me turn is comin' sooner than ye think if ye daenae walk away and pretend ye've nae seen this."

"I won't," she shot back, folding her arms across her chest. "I won't allow you to do this. If it's money you need, I'll... give it to you. But you tell me the truth first. You tell me who you owe and what you owe and why you owe it!"

He lifted his weary gaze to her, the skin sunken around his eyes as if he had not slept since he last saw her. "I owe a huge debt to a gang from the southside. I overheard somethin' I shouldnae have done, and I stupidly warned the person that they were about to be murdered. They left the city, and someone I thought was a friend told the gang that it was me that said somethin'. They couldnae prove it, but they've been punishin' me anyway, ever since. Now, I owe them money each week, without fail, or they'll kill me too. They ken I willnae be able to manage it forever, and, sometimes, I wonder if it might be simpler to just let them get it over with."

Fiona blinked, losing her bluster. She did not know what she had expected, but it was not that.

He has a good heart, she repeated in pensive silence, wondering what on Earth she was supposed to do. She could not allow him to dig up someone who was resting in peace, but nor could she let him die. It would be her fault if she stopped him, and he could not pay what he owed.

"Did you... steal the toys earmarked for the church?" She had to ask, though she could not look at him as she did so.

He made a small, sad sound, partway between a cough and a choke. "I kenned ye'd blame me. I kenned ye'd think of me just as soon as ye saw." He shook his head, running a hand through his fair hair. "I went to the workshop, like ye invited me to. I saw what they'd done, figured I'd be yer only culprit, and made meself scarce. Came here and started what I'd already promised to do. Sort of felt better about it, since I thought ye wouldnae be anywhere near here tonight, with nothin' to bring to the church. But nay, it wasnae me. I swear it on me ma's hedgehog."

"Was it the men you owe money to?"

He shrugged. "Might've been, might've been someone who was passin' and saw an opportunity, might've been the lads who tried to attack yer da four years ago. All I ken for sure is that it wasnae me." He drew in a shaky breath. "I cannae even blame ye for thinkin' it *was* me. What must ye think when ye see me, eh? I'm just a common thief to ye. Someone who'll do anythin' for some coin, even it means takin' from bairns who have so much less."

"I don't think that!" she urged, wringing her hands. "I just... had to be certain, to put my one tiny doubt at ease."

Alastair sniffed and wiped his nose on the back of his hand. "I was supposed to follow in me faither's footsteps, Fiona. I was supposed to be a toymaker, with me own shop, delightin' the bairns. I've dreamed of that for as long as I can remember, and even when everythin' got snatched away, I thought... maybe I'll turn me life around, maybe I'll find a way to pick that dream up and dust it off again. But... it just gets worse, lass. This," he gestured to the fresh grave, "is me lowest ebb, and nay mistake."

Fiona took an anxious step forward, reaching a hand down to him. "Get up."

"Eh?"

"Get up," she repeated softly, wiggling her fingers.

Hesitantly, he took her hand, allowing her to help him to his feet. "Are ye goin' to smack me or somethin'?"

"No." She mustered a smile. "You're going to cover that grave up again and you're going to come to the church with me. We're going to have something warm to eat, and we're going to wait for my pa and Tommy to arrive with toys. Then, we're going to think about how to get you out of this trouble you're in. I have money, I have jewellery, but if that's not enough, we can... talk about helping you leave the city."

And I'll never see you again, her heart sank slowly, like a pebble through oil. *I'll marry Kelvin, I'll start a new life, and... I'l*

I think of you as often as I dare, praying you're well wherever you may be.

He lifted her hand to his lips, kissing it gently. A tingle ran the length of her arm and shivered into her chest, sparking a frantic beat, her stomach fluttering. His mouth was warm and soft, and his eyes, as he raised them up, were shy.

"Turn away," he told her.

She nodded and obeyed, turning around as he shovelled back the dirt he had stolen.

Once Alastair had patted down the grave, leaving it as he had found it, he put his tools in the same bag that had contained stolen goods, and hefted it across his shoulder. He stretched out his hand to Fiona, and she took it without hesitation, the two of them walking back through the foggy, shadowed kirkyard together. But with him at her side, it no longer seemed scary at all. After all, if the boy she had seen *had* been a ghost, he had been a ghost with good intentions, leading her back to someone who needed her help the most.

"Have ye met Bobby?" Alastair asked.

"The little dog?"

He nodded and smiled. "Ye'd think he'd realise it was time to give up, but he doesnae. He just... stays there, standing guard. Makes ye wonder if he kens somethin' we daenae about what happens after." He paused, staring down at the grass. "Can I ask ye a favour, though I ken I've nay right to?"

"Of course," she replied, giving his hand a squeeze.

He sighed wearily. "I want ye to forget ye ever saw me this low."

"Very well," she whispered. And as she watched the fog snaking between old headstones and new, she knew that she would never forget a single thing about him, no matter where he went, or what roads their lives took, away from each other.

Chapter Twelve

The following morning, breakfast at the kitchen table was an unusually quiet affair, everyone lost in their own thoughts. Fiona had not stopped thinking about Alastair, who had accepted something warm to eat at the church, and then made his excuses, vanishing into the night.

Before he left, she had given him the contents of her coin purse, not an inconsiderable sum, and had folded the coins into his hand with a gentle demand, *"Take this and leave the city. Tonight, if you can. Go wherever you'll be out of harm's way and write to me when you get there."*

"I daenae ken how to write, lass, but… I'll find the means," he had replied, pressing another kiss to her hand. And then, he was gone, hopefully as far away as possible, where the gang of thugs could not reach him.

And though it seemed foolish, for she hardly knew him, she missed him already. Missed the promise of the Christmas Eves they might have spent together, and the occasional evenings throughout the year, when he might have stopped by the workshop to offer help.

Better yet, to learn how to make the toys, and pick up and dust off the dream he had spoken so fondly, so desperately about. But just as it was no longer safe to have that workshop, it was no longer safe for Alastair to be in Edinburgh at all.

"What's the matter with the pair of you?" Beryl asked, setting a fresh batch of toast down on the table. "Anyone would think you'd had terrible news."

Donal blinked, emerging from a trance. "Just a lot to consider, love," he said with a sigh. "I'm thinkin' of next year already. I was wonderin' if I might ask Mr. Walker about that room at the back of the shop that he doesnae use for anythin'. It's small, but I can work there, makin' the toys. Then, I could bring 'em up here and put 'em somewhere, and we can… nay, that willnae work. I'll think of somethin', love. I daenae need to worry about it 'til the new year anyway, when I start me makin' again."

"If I have to pick my way around a sea of toys, so be it," Beryl told him, bending to kiss her husband. "Or, I could speak to Mr. Langley about that shed in the yard. No one uses it. He'd say yes if I asked."

Donal pulled a face. "I'll see what Mr. Walker says first." He kissed her back, dancing a slow waltz across a few squares of tile with her, before unleashing a weary groan. "Speakin' of Mr. Walker. I'll be late if ye enchant me with yer wifely wiles a moment longer. Daenae get up to too much mischief today, and save me that last piece of figgy puddin', else I'll pout like a bairn."

"I'll walk you to the shop," Fiona announced, shooting up out of her chair. "I don't feel so good. I need some fresh air."

Beryl blanched, hurrying over to press her palm to her daughter's brow. "Are you feverish again? Did you wrap up warm like I told you to?" She frowned. "You don't feel hot, but if you're not well, perhaps you should return to your bed."

"It's just a headache," Fiona insisted. "The fresh air will fix it."

Beryl nodded uncertainly. "If you're sure."

"I am, Mama." In truth, Fiona needed to clear her head of Alastair, for she had a meeting with her future betrothed in a few days, and she could not afford to be thinking of someone else. A great deal rested on the betrothal being confirmed. Her mother and father tried not discuss it too much when she was present, but she had heard their whisperings in the night— Fiona's marriage would be everyone's security. And Kelvin came from a good family, whatever that meant.

Donal offered his arm to his daughter. "Come along then, wee ducklin'. Ye can have some tea with me in the shop, give me the strength to do somethin' with Lord McIntyre's pocket watch. What possessed him to jump into a loch wearin' it, I daenae ken, but ye cannae expect Lairds to have a jot of sense."

Arm in arm, warm in their coats and gloves and scarves, they stepped out into the crisp morning air. Fiona sucked it deep into her lungs, letting it cool her flushed cheeks, the city bittersweet in the hazy sunlight. Her favourite night of the year was over, and she did not know if she would be allowed to continue next year, or the year after, or the year after. Perhaps, it had been her last year of wandering the Old Town with sacks of toys, sharing stories, gifts, hopes, and morsels of food and drink with people who had become dear to her. The Mrs. Donohues of that world, who looked forward to seeing her.

"I'm proud of us," her father said, filling the companionable silence.

Fiona smiled up at him. "I'm proud of us, too."

"I'll find a new workshop. I'm surprised it wasnae robbed sooner, to be honest," he told her. "But all will be well."

"I have faith in you, Papa. I always have."

He took a breath. "Ye've nay notion of how that encourages me, Fiona. As long as I have the faith of ye and yer ma, I can do anythin'. It willnae be cheap, of course, but... aye, I'll fix this, nay matter what. Ye might find ye have a room I can use when ye venture off and marry the McKintosh boy." He shuddered. "But let's nae speak of that. It's hard enough to think about."

Fiona nodded, holding her tongue. *It will be more difficult than you know.*

Nearing the clockmaker's shop, Donal slowed, his eyes pinching into a squint of confusion as he gazed ahead. Fiona followed his line of sight, her head tilting in a similar sort of bemusement as she saw constables gathered right outside the shop. A small crowd clustered nearby to pry and gossip, their muffled chatter babbling down the street toward the father and daughter.

"Must be the jeweller's," Donal said, shaking his head. "That'll be the third time they've had trouble."

But as the pair got closer, almost to the door, they realised it was not the jeweller's that the constables were there for. The front display of the clockmaker's shop had been cleared of everything but a few stray cogs and nails. Through the glass, it was plain to see the trail of devastation that had been left throughout the shop: a haunting echo of the workshop in the Old Town. Shelves had been pulled away, floorboards pried up, drawers strewn everywhere, locks broken and discarded, every lid of the storage trunks wide open. Even the safe at the back of the shop had been broken into, gutted of every valuable.

"You!" a trembling voice screamed, as someone emerged from the gloom of the ruined shop. "This is the man you want!" Mr. Walker stood in the doorway, pointing a shaky finger straight at Donal. "This man has been stealing from me for years! Now, he has taken everything!"

Donal put up his hands. "I've nae taken anythin', Mr. Walker."

"You stole from me!"

"A few scraps and old pieces of clockwork that served nay purpose, aye, but ye docked me pay for those already," Donal replied, standing in front of Fiona as if he could protect her from what she was hearing.

Two patches of violent red bloomed on the pale of Mr. Walker's sunken cheeks. "You were seen, Donal McVey!" he raged. "You were seen entering my shop late last night with an accomplice joining you shortly after. You were seen leaving with a great sack of goods. And more of your associates came afterwards, finishing what you started. The lady upstairs heard noise and saw it all! You did this! After all I have done for you, you stole it all!"

"Mr. Walker, if I could just speak with ye for a moment. I can explain all of this," Donal said, fear thickening his voice.

Even Fiona could tell that it looked bad. She tried to step around her father, tried to defend him, had the truth ready on the tip of her tongue, but Donal shook his head and whispered, "Leave. Go back to yer ma, tell her what's happened. She'll ken what to do."

"Arrest him!" Mr. Walker howled.

The constables jumped into action, grabbing at Donal as if he had attempted to resist, though he still had his hands up and had not moved at all. One seized him by the scruff of his collar, dragging him to the ground, while another wrenched Donal's arms behind his back. The third constable did not seem to know what to do, standing awkwardly to one side, so it came as a brutal shock when he struck Fiona's father hard in the face.

He's not even fighting you! He's not trying to resist! she wanted to scream, but there was no time for that. Her father needed her help, and it was not going to be an easy situation to explain. But there was one person who might have some notion of how to remedy this, and it was not her mother.

Tommy, she knew. *I have to find Tommy.*

Eyes stinging with tears, her chest on fire with every panicked breath she took, Fiona sprinted across the road and flew down the slope into Princes Street Gardens, heading for the Old Town.

Chapter Thirteen

Breathless and frozen to the bone, a strange grief rising and falling like the cresting waves of a storm-tossed ocean, bringing her back and forth to the brink of tears that refused to spill. She had gone to Tommy's lodgings off Canongate, to no avail.

"He left this mornin' for the port, lass. He'll be away fishin' for the week, 'til the New Year," his wife had explained, looking worried. *"Has somethin' happened? Do ye want to come in for a nip of somethin'? Ye look pale as aught."*

Fiona had refused, shaking with terror, adding only, *"Tell him not to come to the New Town when he comes back. I'll come and find him after the New Year, but you keep him here. You keep him safe."*

Tommy's wife had tried to ask more questions, but Fiona had already taken off, wondering if she could somehow reach the port before Tommy set sail for a week.

It was windy and there seemed to be a storm brewing, but whether or not that would be enough to delay the fishing boat, she did not know.

And if she made it to the port and the boat had gone, she would be even farther from home, and even less sure of what to do next.

So, she returned to the old workshop, pushing through the door that had been broken off its hinges. A pigeon cooed a warning, ruffling its feathers as she entered. The stove had been recently used, still giving off a faint breath of warmth, but that was no surprise. In truth, she was more surprised that beggars and lost souls had not taken the workshop for themselves, to shelter from the biting conditions.

"This isn't right," she whispered, tracing her fingertips across the worn workbench, trying to picture her father sitting on the stool, dedicated to breathing life into whatever creation he held in his hands. The swipe of his paintbrushes, the harsh scent of turpentine and the oddly pleasant, sweet aroma of varnish. The expression upon his face, tongue poking out of his mouth, as he toiled over a nutcracker or a quacking duck or a ginger-haired dolly. The steady tick of clockwork as he tested his more elaborate toys.

All gone. And if her father could not prove his innocence, there might never be a toy in the hands of the worthiest children again.

The children... Her teary eyes widened, a light erupting in the black mist of her mind.

Not bothering to close the door, hoping that those who needed the heat and safety came in and took it, Fiona hurtled out of the passageway and ran as though her life depended on it, tearing down the Royal Mile until she reached the corner of Cowgate.

She eyed the doorways that stretched ahead of her, remembering that Mrs. Donohue's residence had a red door. Though it could not yet have been noon, inebriates swayed and yelled in the streets, whilst ladies in tight bodices, dressed for a party, loitered here and there in pairs or trios, waving at the drunkards who passed. There were children too, crouched at the side of the pavement, playing some sort of game with toys she would have recognized anywhere.

It's a sign, she told herself. *They'll help me. They'll help my papa. They'll tell the magistrates that it's a mistake.*

She crossed over to the red door and knocked, ignoring the burn that seared down the back of her neck, as if someone was watching her. Dressed as she was in her ermine trimmed coat, with a sable tippet around her neck, she stood out in a way she wished she did not.

"What?" a nasty voice seethed as the door flung open, revealing a crooked backed man with glassy eyes and browned teeth.

Fiona swallowed thickly. "Is Mrs. Donohue here?"

"Nay." The man went to slam the door, but Fiona shoved her foot forward, wincing as the door slammed against bone.

"I know she lives here. She's a friend of mine. I need to speak to her," Fiona urged. "My pa is in trouble, and she's the only one who might be able to help."

The man spat at her. "Everyone's pa is in trouble. I'm a pa and I'm in trouble. But I'm nae botherin' honest folk at the crack of dawn."

"It's noon," Fiona replied.

"Aye, well, ye're still botherin' me," the man shot back.

In desperation, Fiona sucked in a breath and shouted as loudly as she could. "Mrs. Donohue? Mrs. Donohue, it's Miss Christmas!"

"Miss who?" the man scoffed.

There was a creak on the stairwell behind the unkind man, followed by footsteps and the slow, arthritic descent of Mrs. Donohue. She hobbled to the door, shoving the man aside. "Get on with ye, Robbie. Daenae be troublin' lasses while yer wife is ready to belt ye." The man retreated sulkily, whilst Mrs. Donohue mustered a cautious smile. "What can I do for ye? Ye ken, ye shouldnae be wanderin' around here dressed like that. Ye'll be robbed blind."

"I… didn't have time to change," Fiona floundered. "I need help, Mrs. Donohue. They arrested my pa for something he didn't do. I need you to come with me, so we can tell the magistrates that they've made a mistake, that my pa was just delivering presents to the church, and that it was someone else who robbed the clock shop."

Mrs. Donohue squinted. "What clock shop?"

"Where my pa works when he's not being Father Christmas," Fiona explained, telling the rest of the story of that morning as quickly as her dry throat would allow. "They took him. they're blaming him, but it wasn't him. If you can gather some people, I'm certain we can convince the magistrates. I'm going to go to the church too and see if they'll offer assistance."

Mrs. Donohue took hold of Fiona's hand, her expression pitying. "I'm tellin' ye this because I've grown fond of ye—it willnae change anythin', lass. Do ye think them fine folk at the magistrates want us Old Town sorts gettin' somethin' for nothin'? If anythin', we'll make it worse. Aye, the constables turn a blind eye on Christmas Eve, but that's because they daenae want to bother themselves with us." She sighed. "Ye might have some fortune with the lads at the church, but if yer pa has been accused of thievin', they might worry they'll be accused of acceptin' stolen goods. It's a mess, aye, but... I daenae think there's a way to fix it, nae on this side of the city. I'm sorry, lass. It was... grand while it lasted, but we've always kenned, deep down, that it would end some day."

"No," Fiona whispered, rubbing her neck to dislodge whatever was blocking her throat, preventing breath from getting into her chest. "No... that can't be it. You... have to help me. They arrested an innocent man!"

Mrs. Donohue shook her head. "Look at where ye are, lass. What ye're sufferin' is what half of us have suffered." She patted Fiona's hand. "I'm sorry, lass. There really is nothin' I can do. Ye'll just have to pray and hope, like the rest of us."

"But... but..." Fiona spluttered, every argument withering away before it could form. Of course, she could say that her father did a good, charitable thing for these people, but he never asked anything in return. Indeed, asking for something in return negated the charitable nature of it, and she did not want to tarnish those wonderful, awful, life-altering Christmas Eves. And how could she say that her father was any different to other fathers who had been arrested, perhaps just as innocent? It would be throwing mud in Mrs. Donohue's face.

"Try the fellas at the church," Mrs. Donohue repeated. "Ye're dressed nice, ye speak nice, they ken yer da; ye might be lucky."

As the door closed in Fiona's face, she turned and shambled away, a shard of ice in her heart. Part of her wanted to make demands, to tell these people that her father *was* different, and they were cruel to refuse to help. She wanted to scorn them for eagerly accepting toys, but telling her the equivalent of "you're on your own" now that she needed something from them.

She fed off that ember of anger, letting it spur her on before she lost hope all together. Moving to the next door, she knocked and immediately had the door slammed in her face. At the next door, a younger woman shrugged and said it was none of her concern. On and on, Fiona knocked as if the clock had rewound to Christmas Eve, but instead of a sack of gifts she had her heart and her hope in her hands, begging for mercy.

She supposed she should have known that the magic of Christmas would not stretch. Many of those she pleaded with did not even seem to recognise her, their former pleasantries transforming into wariness and an eagerness for the conversation to be over. She was not Miss Christmas anymore, she was just some reasonably well-to-do young woman, wearing furs none of them could afford, asking for more than they were willing to give. She had returned to the sort of person they had vowed to hate.

"If I was one of you, you would help," she whispered, remembering something Alastair had said, a long time ago.

***

By the time evening fell, Fiona had been wandering and knocking on doors for hours, no longer affected by the outright refusals or insults that came her way.

She bore them with a nod and an apology, moving on to receive more of the same. But her legs were tired and her stomach was growling, prompting her to head in the direction of her very last hope: Greyfriars Kirk.

She knew she should return home to inform her mother, who would be beside herself with worry, but she could not stand the thought of going back to those warm, lovely apartments without a solution.

After all, if something happened to her father, if he could not convince the magistrates of his innocence, then there was no telling how long they might have those lovely apartments for.

The gates to the kirkyard squealed as she entered, frost glinting on the grass. From his usual spot, Bobby lifted his head to see who was coming, and lowered it again.

"Good evening, Bobby," Fiona said, walking hesitantly toward the grave. She crouched down and offered her hand for the little terrier to sniff. And once she was certain he would not bite, she gave him a tender scratch between the ears, soothed by the sensation of fur beneath her fingertips.

Leaving him to his night watch, she padded over to the church, covering her mouth with her hand as a yawn stretched her face. A few votives flickered beyond the church windows, the bright light a welcome greeting to hopeless travellers.

But as she reached the heavy doors and tugged on the iron ring that served as a handle, the door would not budge. Wondering if it had somehow frozen stuck in the cold, she braced her foot against the other door and heaved with all her might, her back almost horizontal as she pulled and pulled. But the door stayed shut. Locked. Only the votives inside.

Surely not, she told herself. It was a church; it had to be open. Moreover, it was a church with lit candles inside—to leave it unattended was downright foolish.

She banged on the door, shouting, "Is anyone there? I need to speak with the clergyman!" She thumped her fist harder, hearing it echo inside. "Excuse me! I need to speak with someone!"

The votives taunted her. No one was in there. No one was coming.

Well, I shall just have to stay all night, until someone does come, she promised angrily, hoping that the clergymen had merely gone home for their dinner and would return soon. But she did not know what time it was. Perhaps, it was long past the hour for dinner. Her own might even be waiting on the table, stone cold as her mother watched the door, waiting for her family to breeze into the warmth as they always did.

Sitting down on the cold steps, glancing over at Bobby, it somehow felt like no time had passed at all since she was last there, in that exact spot. Maybe, it had been a terrible dream. Maybe, she had fallen asleep while waiting for her father and Tommy to arrive with the toys, and the day she had just endured had not happened at all.

"Alastair," she whispered, cursing herself. He could have helped, he *would* have helped explain the truth, but she had sent him away with all the coin in her purse, and she did not know where he was.

Nor did she have any way of corresponding, to let him know what had taken place.

Getting wearily to her feet, rubbing her leaden legs, she set off through the kirkyard, meandering by the silver light of the moon. Where she could, she read the names on the headstones, trying to imagine what the owners might have looked like, sounded like; what they had dreamed of, what they had enjoyed most about life.

She thought of the pale-faced boy, still not entirely convinced that he had not been a ghost, and tried to follow the path she had taken the previous night, chasing him through the kirkyard. But everything looked different and alike, all at once.

Pacing around a yew tree that seemed somewhat familiar, she froze and listened to the cemetery around her, uncertain of what was real and what was her imagination. She could have sworn she heard that same, awful sawing sound that had brought her to Alastair the previous night.

Is that why the clergymen aren't here? She listened harder, but the sound did not disappear. *Do they know that people are digging up the dead?*

She crept towards the sound, realising too late that it was a terrible idea. If she stumbled upon a resurrectionist, they would be inclined to silence her however they could. And her stiff legs were in no condition to run anywhere fast.

But just as sanity was about to reclaim her body and turn her around, she saw him. The resurrectionist, half-swallowed up by a grave, throwing dirt into a messy pile at the grave's edge. On the headstone of the poor soul who was about to be hauled from their resting place, she saw the shine of varnish and the rudimentary spikes of enthusiastic but unskilled hands. A perfectly, beautifully ugly little hedgehog.

"Alastair?" her voice trembled as she called out to him, stumbling down the slope towards him.

He stopped dead, hunched over. He did not turn. It was as if he hoped she would not see him if he just stayed still, though it was obviously too late for that.

"You're not supposed to be here," she said, her breath catching. "You're supposed to be far away. You pretty much promised you wouldn't do anything like this again, so... what are you doing? Why are you here?"

With a ragged sigh, he clambered out of the grave and perched on the lip, kicking his legs like he was sitting on a pier instead of someone else's earthly bed. "I tried." He dragged his sleeve across a glistening brow. "I couldnae do it."

"Why not?"

"I'm sorry about yer faither's shop," was all he said in reply, hanging his head. It was at that moment that Fiona noticed the swelling and bruising on his face. One eye was swollen almost shut, his lip split, a shiner on his cheek... an echo of the way he had looked when they first met.

Shock squeezed the breath from Fiona's lungs. "How do you know about my father's shop?"

"Because I was on me way to the stagecoach, ready to leave, but I just *had* to go back to that stupid workshop one more time. I saw them in there, heard them talkin' about yer faither's shop—one of them kenned where it was, and kenned there'd be plenty worth stealin'. I followed them all the way to the New Town, I tried to stop them, and they took everythin' anyway. Took everythin' from yer da's shop, took the money ye gave me. So, aye, I paid me debt for this week, but... I'm still here. And I'm doin' this because I really have nay other choice now. I... wanted to at least give back what ye gave me."

Fiona wanted to believe every word. She willed herself to, yet there was something too strange in Alastair's voice. A tightness, a quickness, a rambling quality, like a child explaining all the reasons they had not stolen the jam, whilst wearing it across their face. Nor could he look at her, as if conscious of having that telltale jam somewhere within his expression, betraying him.

"Alastair," she said softly. "Be honest with me."

His head snapped up, his good eye narrowing. "I *am* bein' honest with ye. Look at me face if ye daenae believe me. They beat me black and blue 'cause I tried to stop them."

"But did you follow them to my father's shop, or did you lead them there?" She hated herself for asking, but it weighed too heavy upon her thoughts to stay silent. "I'm not saying you wanted to lead them there, but could it be that you were forced to?"

His lip curled, nostrils flaring. "Of course ye'd think that of me, same as ye thought I stole all them toys from the workshop. Ye probably gave me all the coin ye had just to get me away from ye." He reached for his coat, discarded at the side of the grave, and draped it over his shoulders. He winced as he moved, suggesting a more elaborate patchwork of bruises beneath his shirt and jacket. "I'm still just an urchin to ye, am I nae?"

"I want to know what happened, that's all," she replied evenly. "It's important. My father was arrested this morning."

Alastair's eyes widened to the whites. "What?"

"Mr. Walker, the owner of the shop, blamed my father. There was a witness—some nosey woman in the apartments above. She saw my father and Tommy go in to fetch the toys he had hidden there and emerge with the sack. Then, I assume she saw those thugs you're referring to, a while later. Of course, she didn't bother to summon help at the time; she just waited until morning so she could point the finger at my papa. Either way, she was wrong, and now my father is in dire trouble. *That* is why I need to know what happened. Every detail, even if it's hard to say."

He crumpled like a paper doll, folding in on himself, his forehead practically touching his knees as he held his head in his hands. "Nay... nay, nay, nay..." he hissed under his breath. "Yer poor da."

"What did you do, Alastair?" Fiona held her breath, bracing for the reply as if it would come in the form of a fist to her gut.

Shaking his head, gripping fistfuls of his hair, he sobbed his answer, "They... threatened ye, lass. They said they'd wait 'til next Christmas Eve if they had to, but they'd... snatch ye if I... didnae tell them where the shop was. They kenned all about yer da. Kenned he worked for some fine clockmaker. Kenned... there'd be valuables, but nae where the shop was, or how to get in from the back. I daenae ken how they had so much information, but... I promise ye, I was on me way to the stagecoach. Was waitin' for the stagecoach, truth be told. That's where... they found me. They dragged me off, beat me half to death, and when I still wouldnae tell them what they wanted to ken, they... used ye. I believed them. Still do, and I'd tell them again if it meant sparin' ye."

"Alastair, no..." she choked, her worst fears like ghosts, clawing at her flesh, chilling her to her core. "You... you shouldn't have done that. I wasn't going to be there next Christmas Eve anyway! Alastair, no! Oh no, no..."

He tilted his head to the side, peering at her with narrowed eyes. "What do ye mean, ye were nae goin' to be there next year anyway?"

"I... I am..." her throat tightened, a hand of guilt squeezing tight, "... I am to be married. Betrothed, at least, but a wedding will follow soon after. A good man from a good family. You... shouldn't have told them, Alastair. It wouldn't have mattered. They wouldn't have been able to get to me."

Anger flared in Alastair's summer sky eyes, changing their season to bitter winter. "Ye're to be married?"

Fiona nodded. *But my heart is reaching elsewhere. I fear it has been since I was twelve years old, saved by a boy who loved Christmas so much, and vanished before my eyes. I boy that, for years, I thought was a dream. The most precious dream.* She could not say so out loud, did not dare to, not with everything hanging in the balance. Indeed, if her father remained imprisoned, her marriage to Kelvin might be the only saving grace that her and her mother had, to keep them from destitution.

"And ye didnae think that was somethin' ye should've mentioned?" His voice carried barbs that lodged in Fiona's skin, stinging all the way to her heart. "Yer da might be safe in his bed, right now, if ye'd said somethin'. I might have left earlier, might nae have waited to see ye got to the New Town safely, after I left ye at the kirk, if I'd kenned ye were to be wed to a good man from a good family." He spat the last words, each one fizzing with venom.

"Don't say that," she pleaded, scrunching her eyes shut. "Don't put blame at my door."

"What, like ye've just put blame at mine?" he shot back, getting to his feet. "I thought I was protectin' ye, but I see now that I shouldnae have bothered. Ye daenae need protection from a thief, a body snatcher, a criminal like me when ye've a "good man" waitin'. To think, I've thought of ye every night for four years. I bet ye havenae even thought of me once."

Fiona's eyes flew open. "That's not true, Alastair. I thought of you so often. *Think* of you so often. That's not fair! Marrying Kelvin isn't something I asked for, any more than you being a thief is something you asked for." She shivered violently, though she did not know if it was the cold or his accusation. "But we are losing sight of the important thing here—my father is in trouble, and you might be one of the only people who can help. You can tell the magistrates the truth. If I do, Tommy does, my ma does, and you do, he will be freed in no time; I am certain of it."

"Me word means nothin'," he replied icily. "I'm a thief and a wrong'un to them, as I am to ye. If I could, I would help him, but... I'm nae any sort of hope for him. Tommy willnae be, either. He's been in gaol before. His word willnae mean aught. Believe me, I've seen it a thousand times. The only voices they might listen to are yers and yer ma's, but it'll depend how highly the magistrates think of this Mr. Walker. If he has them in his pocket, ye can scream 'til ye're blue in the face and it'll nae make a difference."

Fiona's frozen legs thawed, and she ran to Alastair, seizing hold of his arms. "I can't do this alone. The more people my father has on his side, the more they will *have* to listen. Is that not the nature of justice? They will not be able to ignore the voices of many."

"Ye've been among us for four years now," he said, staring down into her eyes, "and ye still daenae understand anythin'. Here, there is nay justice, and yer faither isnae a high-and-mighty laird or gentleman. He's practically one of us too, and they'll treat him as such. It doesnae matter if ye're innocent if ye're lowly. To them, ye were born guilty, they just havenae pinned a crime to ye yet."

A sob wracked Fiona's chest, her fingernails sinking into Alastair's arms. "Please..."

"I'm sorry." He pried her hands away from him and held them for a moment, slowly peeling away her gloves. As he balled them up and stuffed them in her coat pocket, Fiona too shocked to move, he brought her bare hands to his lips and pressed a slow, painful kiss to her pale skin. She closed her eyes for a moment, her stomach knotting, her heart racing. And when he drew back and her eyes opened once more, he continued to stare at her hands, as if seeing something etched in secret writing upon the blue strands of her veins. His voice softened as he said, "I hope this Kelvin of yers can do what I cannae. Because yer faither *is* a good man, and it'd be a cryin' shame if... he rots in gaol for doin' a fine deed. Now, if ye'll excuse me, I need to leave before I say somethin' I'll regret."

He dropped her hands and walked off, breaking into a run before she could grab him or halt him or even call him back. The darkness swallowed him up, the kirkyard devouring any sound of his retreating footfalls, leaving Fiona entirely alone beside an open grave, her heart in pieces.

At that moment, the moonlight caught the sheen of varnish, drawing her eye to the hedgehog he had forgotten to take. And though she knew she should not, and had no right, she picked it up off the headstone, cradled it in her bare hands, letting the spikes dig into her flesh, and made her own way out of the kirkyard.

If Alastair wanted it back, he would have to face her again.

As she walked through the Old Town that had refused to aid her, haunted by the pain in Alastair's voice as she had told him of her imminent betrothal and the bruises that he had gained because of her.

Not to mention the guilt that simmered in her breast because she had not been honest and now her father was imprisoned, the tears she had been fighting all day finally came. Pulling her gloves from her pocket, she used them in place of a handkerchief, dabbing her eyes as the tears spilled at will, great sobs heaving from her throat, aching in her chest.

I need my mama, she knew, walking faster toward the bridge that traversed the city, joining the Old Town to the New. She rarely used it with her father, preferring the cover of the park, but there seemed little point in being furtive now.

Dipping her chin to her chest, skin whipped by the wind that tunnelled across the bridge, she was almost at the other side, almost within reach of her home, when something Alastair said came rushing back: *"I might have left earlier, might nae have waited to see ye got to the New Town safely, after I left ye at the kirk."*

Slowly, she turned, squinting back at the gloom of the Old Town. There, standing at the threshold to the bridge, was a lone figure in a familiar coat. A stolen coat.

Despite vanishing again, he had come to ensure that she returned to her side of the city safely. This time, however, he had left footprints, firmly embedded in the thick snow of her heart. And this time, she knew it would be the last time she ever saw him.

Chapter Fourteen

Edinburgh, 1861

Though Christmas Eve had come once again to the city of Edinburgh, the beautiful constant that Fiona had looked forward to every year of her life, everything had changed for her and her mother.

In twelve months, their world had turned on its head, blow after blow battering the lifeboat they still clung to, together.

The morning after Donal's arrest, a letter had arrived by express messenger from the family of Kelvin McKintosh. It had been brutal in its simplicity; the first sign of things to come: *After sensible consideration, we have decided that it would not be in our interest to meet with you next week. Please do not respond. Yours Sincerely, Alfred McKintosh, Esq.*

In those first twenty-four hours, the rug was pulled from beneath Beryl and Fiona, casting them adrift.

Both knew what it meant to lose the prospect of that betrothal.

Both knew, as they had sat across from one another at the kitchen table where they had revelled in their "Yule" feast and had dined on a smaller banquet just two days prior, on Christmas Day, that it would not be long before they had to relinquish the place that they called home. And with their home, everything that, unwittingly, they had taken for granted.

In truth, they had held onto the apartments for two months, enduring the worst of a terrible winter in the shelter of that sanctuary.

They had scrimped on coal and wood, huddling together beneath thick blankets, sleeping in the same bed to share heat, but once the end of February arrived, their landlord offered his apologies with a notice of eviction.

By the first week of March, they had sold the majority of their belongings, holding onto only what was necessary, and had made a miserable journey across the bridge to the Old Town.

They had been there ever since, residing in one tiny room in a tenement building on Canongate, across the hallway from Tommy, his wife Olwyn, and his darling children.

Wind-whipped and breathless, Fiona tore up the creaking staircase of the tenement building, taking the steps two at a time. Reaching the eaves, she burst through the door she knew would not be unlocked, throwing back the hood of her cloak as she skidded to a halt. "Mama, it's snowing!" she cried, grinning from ear to ear. "It just started now! You have to come and see!"

Intently watching a pot that hung over the fireplace, Beryl turned and smiled. "I can see, you silly goose."

She chinned toward the small, soot-stained window that possessed—in Fiona's opinion—one of the finest views in Edinburgh. "I've been waiting an age for you to run in like that. You've no notion of how it cheers my heart."

"Come on." Fiona dragged her mother by the arm, pulling her towards the window. It was a hinged window that opened outward like a door, and though it was freezing out there, Fiona pushed it wide so they could stick their heads out and try to catch the cold flakes on their tongues.

A blast of icy air swept in, and Beryl closed her eyes, wearing an expression of delight as the wind tousled her hair and cooled her red cheeks. "That's nice," she murmured. "It'll take all night to make the room warm again, but… that's very nice."

"I saw Olwyn in the street," Fiona said, resting her cheek on her mother's shoulder. "She asked what time we're coming across the hallway. I said five o'clock, so I can play with the bairns and make myself useful before I venture out."

Beryl nodded. "I should have the pudding steamed by then."

"It smells wonderful," Fiona encouraged, inhaling deeply. The blended aroma of fresh, crisp snow, woodsmoke, and spiced fruit pudding warmed her very soul, so that if she closed her eyes, she could imagine that she was back in the New Town apartments, and nothing had changed at all.

And that her father would walk in at any moment, tired but happy after a day in the clockmaker's shop, to kiss his wife in that way that used to embarrass Fiona, before he embraced his daughter.

"It was terribly kind of Mrs. Ogilvy to present me with the pudding" Beryl said, withdrawing from the window. "I wasn't expecting anything at all, but she's a good woman, Mrs. Ogilvy. We're... very lucky."

Fiona forced a smile. "Very lucky."

They had vowed to one another, when they left the other side of the city, that they would make the best of every day in their new lives. Some days, it was harder than others, but Fiona knew that neither of them had expected Christmas Eve to be easy.

Her mother's eyes were rimmed with red, dark circles like bruises underneath, and though, if asked, she would insist it was because of the smoke getting in her eyes, Fiona knew better.

It would be almost a year to the day since they had last seen Donal, and though they petitioned the magistrates month after month, repeating his innocence until they were, indeed, blue in the face, it seemed unlikely that they would see him again, anytime soon.

The courts had labelled him a thief, sentencing him to ten years in the gaol, and they did not like to be told they had judged wrongly.

"Indeed, she has invited us to tea on New Year's Day," Beryl said, distracting Fiona from gloomy thoughts.

"Who has?"

"Mrs. Ogilvy." Beryl smiled. "I think she gets lonely."

Fiona paused. "I think I am tending to my duties on New Year's Eve, so I might look like a girl who hasn't slept all night, but that sounds delightful." She walked to her mother and put her arms around her. "I'm glad you two found one another."

"As am I." Beryl turned and kissed her daughter on the forehead.

In truth, Mrs. Ogilvy had been something of a miracle, though Fiona did not entirely know how her mother had met the old, wealthy widow. All she *did* know was that, on the second week of March, her mother had come home and informed her that she had found employment with an elderly lady who lived alone in a rather splendid townhouse on the Royal Circus. An elderly lady called Mrs. Ogilvy, who paid Beryl enough to afford the tiny lodgings in return for general housekeeping and the cooking of light meals, but was always sending her off with parcels of food and, on occasion, delicacies like the steamed fruit pudding that was, at present, singing in the pot.

"Doesn't she have any family visiting for the festive season?" Fiona asked, parting ways with her mother. She slipped behind a partition formed of hung blankets and shed her day clothes, rummaging through an oak trunk for her evening uniform.

"She had no children," her mother called back. "I think her great-nephew is visiting on Christmas Day, but that is all. I don't think there *is* anyone else, no."

"Are you working on Christmas Day?" Fiona tried to keep the disappointment out of her voice, but she could hear the tightness of it in every word.

"Just until luncheon, then her great-nephew is taking her out to dine."

Fiona pulled on woollen trousers and cinched them with a cracked leather belt, stuffing her shirt tails into the waist. "Olwyn wanted to know if we would join them for dinner—that's why I was asking."

"Oh!" Beryl sounded pleased. "Tell her we will! Or, I can tell her when we see her in an hour, I suppose."

Fiona smiled. "It's all that steam getting up your nose and into your brain. It's fogging your mind."

"But doesn't it smell marvellous?"

Fiona took another deep inhale. "It does. Worth the fog."

"Where are you tonight?"

"Calton Cemetery."

Her mother grumbled quietly. "Did Tommy say you could borrow his pistol again? You know I don't like you being out there without a pistol."

"He said he'd bought me my own, as a Christmas gift." Fiona smiled, waiting for the imminent protest.

"He did not!"

Fiona stifled a laugh as she shrugged on her jacket. "He did, I swear!"

"You're teasing me again, aren't you? Don't you know it's not kind to tease your poor mother?"

Fiona let her laugh bubble freely from her lips. "Fine, he isn't giving me my own, but he's said I can borrow it again. Actually, he said I might as well have it, since he has no use for it, but I like the excuse of going across the hall to see the little ones."

"As if you need an excuse," her mother said brightly. "I don't know why we bother closing our doors anymore."

"Because Mr. Forrester is strange," Fiona reminded her mother. "Although, I haven't seen him in weeks. Have you?"

"Last week," Beryl confirmed. "Caught him trying to trap a rat. I think he roasted it and ate it."

"Now who's teasing who?"

"I'm quite serious!"

Fiona stuck her head out from behind the partition. "You're not?"

"I promise you. I saw him trap the rat, then he took it into his room, and there was a nasty smell coming out of there shortly afterwards. A lot of smoke, too." Beryl shuddered. "Still, we mustn't judge. Next year, *we* might be having roasted rat for Christmas dinner."

Fiona laughed. "Not if Mrs. Ogilvy has anything to say about it."

"Well, yes, I suppose you're right." Beryl smiled and resumed her watch over the steamed pudding, waiting for the perfect moment to pluck it out of the pot. A moment later, she glanced back at her daughter, as if she had not seen Fiona properly the first time. "Goodness, I'll never get used to seeing you like that."

Fiona did a twirl, jamming a cloth cap down on her head and tucking her hair beneath it. "You should try it. It's comfortable."

"I think I shall keep to my dresses and skirts, but thank you." Beryl sighed and sat upon on a low stool, reaching down to massage her ankles. "I wish you would agree to come and work with me at Mrs. Ogilvy's house, or at least allow me to ask her if she knows of anyone in need of a maid."

Fiona removed the cap and let her hair fall loose. "Mama, we've discussed this. I would be a hopeless maid and, as it turns out, I'm rather good at protecting the dead. I have a gift for scenting out resurrectionists and they seem to be remarkably scared of me."

She could not admit that, though she did like the satisfaction of guarding those who could not guard themselves, there was another reason she had begun that line of work: the hope of one day seeing Alastair again.

But in the nine months she had been employed as a protector of graves, she had not seen hide nor hair of him. It gave her peace, in a way, to know he had not returned to body snatching, but that did not mean her eyes did not search for him in the dark, regardless.

"Well, I wish you had a gift for polishing silver instead," her mother muttered, stifling a yawn.

Fiona shrugged. "Guarding graves pays better."

It was something she had learned early on, during their first month in the Old Town. She had desperately tried to attain work, accepting any employment she could, only to receive a pittance in return. Her mother had tried to insist that it did not matter, that her employment would be enough, but Fiona had been determined to lighten her mother's burdens.

That was when she had overheard Tommy talking about someone he knew, who was looking for a boy to guard a grave.

"I know a boy who would be perfect," she had told Tommy, gaining a wary look in return.

"It better nae be that Alastair lad," he had replied, inflicting an unknowing sting to Fiona's heart.

"It's not. It's someone I met whilst I was working at the market. He's capable, he's punctual, and he won't let anyone get away with stealing a body from a grave," Fiona had insisted, trying hard not to think of Alastair. She had assumed they might cross paths in the Old Town but they never had.

Tommy had shrugged. "Tell him to go to Greyfriars at nine o'clock on Friday night. He'll have to spend the whole night there, so make sure ye tell him to bring a lantern or somethin' to warm himself. I'll tell me friend I've got someone, but he'd better nae let me down, Fiona. There's good money in this."

At half-past-eight on that Friday night, Fiona had dressed in boy's clothing that she had stolen from a washing line, realising the irony, and had slipped out of the lodgings whilst her mother slept, venturing through the dangers of the Old Town to reach Greyfriars.

She had greeted Bobby and scratched his head, waiting for her client to arrive. At nine o'clock, an old man had shambled through the gates. She had approached him, lowering the pitch of her voice, and told him that she would be guarding the grave that night.

"I'll pay you sixpence in the morning, once I've seen the grave for myself," the man had told her, startling her with the sum. "If you do well, I can give you two shillings a week, for six nights. I watch my son on a Sunday night."

She had jumped at the chance and had remained steadfast at that grave for six weeks, after which time the old man had informed her that his son was no longer of any interest to body snatchers. She was relieved of her duties with an additional shilling for her valiant efforts.

However, word had spread that she was particularly vigilant at her work, and since May of that year, she had rarely been without a grave to guard, usually until the owner of the grave was no longer "fresh." All the while, her clients believed she was a boy, and she was not inclined to correct them. She had even contemplated cutting her hair, but stuffing it under the cap seemed to work well enough.

"Do you know who you're guarding tonight?" Beryl asked, setting a small teakettle directly onto the fire. "Is that a macabre question? I never know."

Fiona pulled up a stool and warmed her hands against the heat of the blaze. "A young woman. A lady, I think." She frowned into the flames, considering all the young women of the Old Town who had died without a resting place of their own, tossed in with the rest of the "riff-raff" in a paupers' grave. "Not much older than me. Nine-and-ten when she passed, I believe."

A choked sound lodged in Beryl's throat. "Oh goodness... that's awful. That poor girl." She turned and smacked her daughter lightly on the arm. "Don't you dare even think about joining her! Promise me you will fire that pistol if you have to!"

"I've become quite a good shot," Fiona teased, circling an arm around her mother. "I promise, I'll be home before you leave for Mrs. Ogilvy's, as always."

And whilst you're at the townhouse, I'm going to buy us something delicious for our very own Christmas Day feast, she vowed silently, knowing that tomorrow was going to be just as hard as Christmas Eve for both of them.

As they sat together by the warmth of the fire, with the snow coming down beyond the sooty window, the strangest, most glorious sound began to across from Tommy and Olwyn's lodgings. The latter's sweet soprano voice enchanted the smoky air with the opening lyrics of "Once in Royal David's City," joined soon after by the resonant tenor of her husband, Tommy. To look at him, no one would have thought he was a gifted singer, and they would have been sorely mistaken.

A few moments later, a rich baritone added itself to the music of the carol, seemingly coming from strange Mr. Forrester's room. Gradually, with courage and festive cheer, voices echoed up from the floors below, songbirds and caterwaulers alike, adding their instrument to the carol until the entire tenement seemed to be singing as one.

The fine hairs stood on end on the backs of Fiona's forearms, her skin tingling into goosebumps as she listened in awe, her heart so full she thought it might burst.

And though she only had a passable singing voice, she let the words flow out of her mouth and clung to her mother, who finally added the most exquisite soprano to the song.

Tears from an ancient well of wonder coursed down their cheeks as they sang with all their might, holding tight to one another, their hearts and souls lightened for as long as it lasted.

It appeared they were not alone in relishing the magic of the moment, for as the words of the carol came to end, someone far below began the first verse of "I Saw Three Ships." A livelier tune to further rouse the spirits of all those who shared one building, making something glorious, together, out of nothing but the magic of Christmas and good will to all.

Chapter Fifteen

Watching the snowflakes tumbling down over Edinburgh, Fiona sat beneath a lean-to made of sticks and a wide square of canvas that she had brought with her, admiring the sight. The world had become peaceful once more, her heart still warm from the tenement carols, and the Christmas Eve supper she had shared with her mother, Tommy, Olwyn, and their four children.

A lantern glowed at her side, illuminating the waxed paper parcel her mother had sent her off with.

Fiona knew she ought to save it for later, but with her mood so bright and her spirits so high, she could not resist peeling back the paper to get to the slice of steamed pudding inside.

It was still warm, the taste of spices and dried fruit and sugar exploding on her tongue as she took her first bite.

It was the flavour of the past, reminding her of happy years with her family at one table, but there was hope, too, somewhere amongst the currants and raisins and candied peel. Hope that, one day, they would sit at a table together again—her, her mother, and her father, and Tommy's family too, no doubt.

This isn't so bad, she mused, leaning politely against the headstone of the young woman she was guarding. She glanced down and traced her fingertips gently across the engraved epitaph: *Here Lies Georgette Arbroath. Beloved Daughter. Born December 21st 1841. Died December 19th 1861. An Angel Made Flesh, Fly Home Now.*

"I'm sorry," Fiona whispered, crumbling some of the steamed pudding onto the freshly turned earth of the grave. "I don't know that I'm allowed to say this, but... a belated happy birthday to you. I hope you're... well, wherever you are. Goodness, what if you're looking at me right now, dropping crumbs on your grave? I mean it in kindness, I promise."

She looked back out at the falling snow, describing the scene to the young woman, as she did for all those whose graves she watched over.

Although, during her employment as a protector of the dead, she had seen some things in the eerie dark of the kirkyards and cemeteries of Edinburgh that had convinced her that, sometimes, the dead like to linger for a while.

Ghosts and entities that, up until then, had been well-intentioned, keeping to themselves, wandering at their leisure, mostly unaware that Fiona was observing.

"It's beautiful, but I'd be lying if I said it wasn't cold," she said. "There's nothing like coming in from the cold, though, is there? Sitting by a fire, thawing, maybe with some toast and butter and a hot cup of tea. Did you like the snow? I think you might have done. You seem like the sort of person who would. My sort of person."

She liked to imagine the people she guarded, and the longer she guarded them, the more stories she learned about them from the family who visited and paid her when her night watch was over.

However, the lady beside her was unusual, for it had been a servant of the household who had met her at the gates of Calton Cemetery.

Yet, even he had seemed tearful, his voice choking as he had shown her to the grave and explained the fee and payment. It was most peculiar for the servants to be sad about one of their "superiors," confirming that she must have been an exceptional young woman. A true angel made flesh, now returned home.

"What was your favourite carol?" Fiona asked, trying to decide. "I'll hum a few, but I won't subject you to my singing."

Pulling her blanket tighter around herself, she began to hum the tune to "O Come All Ye Faithful," pausing here and there to finish off the delicious slice of steamed pudding. No storm suddenly brewed out of nowhere and no harsh wind whipped at her face, so she had to assume that Miss Georgette Arbroath was enjoying her selection.

Indeed, she was just about to chance a quiet rendition of "Silent Night," when the violent snap of a twig erupted like a musket shot, splintering her peace and quiet.

Instinct took over, driving her hand toward the pepper-box pistol that lay in her lap.

She gripped the butt of the pistol tightly and peered down the short barrel, turning it toward the sound, though the blood rushing in her ears drowned out everything else. Still, her eyesight was crystal clear. A figure in a black cloak had just emerged from between two sentinel oaks, the bottom half of their face covered by a mask, while a low hood concealed the upper half. They carried a shovel on their shoulder, their intentions clear.

Without hesitation, thinking only of Georgette Arbroath, Fiona fired the pistol. The lead ball merged into the darkness, as Fiona held her breath and quickly rotated the chamber, in case she needed to fire again. Usually, a warning shot was enough, but she was not willing to risk waiting.

A yelp went up, the figure's hand flying to their shoulder. A guttural groan of pain followed, concluding with a sharp hiss through clenched teeth. "Is that... how ye greet an old friend? Mercy, lass, ye've changed!" the figure shouted across the gap that separated them.

Shock shuddered so viscerally through Fiona's veins that she almost dropped the pistol. She knew that voice. She had thought of it so often over the past year, listening out for it in crowds or down alleyways or in the kirkyards where she held her vigils, but never hearing it.

"Don't come any closer!" Fiona yelled back, finding her voice as she lumbered to her feet.

But Alastair did, walking forward with one hand raised in a gesture of surrender. "I daenae mean ye any harm, lass. I saw ye and I wanted to speak with ye, that's all."

"With a shovel on your shoulder?" Fiona sniffed, wondering if they had simply not been in the same cemeteries at the same time, or if he had fallen on harder times once more, and had returned to the wicked art of body snatching. "I mean it, stay where you are."

He kept coming, pulling down his mask and pushing down his hood to reveal the face she had missed so much. "I was gardenin'. Do ye nae like to garden of a Christmas Eve night?"

Her stomach roiled, her heart beating out of rhythm, her palm clammy as she readjusted her grip on the pistol butt. She had waited for months, seen his face in a thousand other faces, only to be disappointed. Why had he come on that night, when her spirits were high, with that blasted shovel over his shoulder? The last thing she wanted was to fight with him again, considering how they had parted ways. But... she had a duty to do.

"I struck you once," she said, her shock transforming into courage as she stood in front of the headstone, as if it were actually Georgette Arbroath behind her. "A graze of the shoulder, easily healed. But if you—or anyone, for that matter—attempts to touch the young lady I am protecting, I should warn you, I rarely miss what I'm aiming for."

Don't make me do it, she prayed, steadying her breaths. *I've waited a year for this. Please, don't do something we'll both regret.*

To her dismay and delight, he took a step closer.

Chapter Sixteen

To Fiona's surprise and horror, Alastair veered away from her, trudging further down the slope until he reached a crooked yew tree. In front of it was a large iron mortsafe, caging in an upsettingly small headstone.

The ground did not look like it had been freshly turned for burial, yet Alastair took a key out of his pocket, twisted it in the hefty lock that held the mortsafe closed and lifted the long grille lid. Standing inside it, right on top of the grave, he began, jarringly, to dig.

"That doesn't mean you can go snatching anyone else, either!" Fiona ran forward, the pistol shaky in her hand. Her eyes searched the tiny, rounded headstone, but it merely said, *"Lost Treasures."* Nevertheless, she could imagine what was buried beneath. "Do you get more money if they're children? Is that it?"

Alastair had the gall to laugh, and kept right on digging.

"Stop that!" Fiona grabbed his arm, spinning him around. "Those are babies, Alastair. Don't you dare."

Alastair leaned on the handle of his shovel, grinning. "There's nothin' in here. I bought the plot, put the headstone and mortsafe up meself. Left it for a few weeks, but no one came diggin', so I kenned it was right for me plans. Turns out, resurrectionists have *some* morality."

"What?" She blinked at him.

"Ye'll see," he told her, driving the shovel into the ground once more. "And if ye're nae goin' to shoot me again, can ye put that pistol down? Ye're makin' me nervous."

She lowered the weapon and retreated back to her post to watch him. He worked quickly, his powerful arms shifting the dirt with ease. He looked well, as if he had enjoyed better fortune since they last saw one another. He must have done, if he had been able to afford a headstone and a mortsafe and a grave that had nothing inside.

At length, the contents of the grave began to reveal itself. The lumpy rise of what appeared to be sacks, wrapped in black tarpaulins, filled the hole he had made. Fiona shuddered, terrified of what might be inside those sacks. Had he taken to rat-catching or the crude disposal of bodies that needed to disappear? She remembered the gang who kept threatening him—had threatened her, too—and wondered if he had agreed to work for them to save himself.

Curiosity led her back to the strange grave, though she checked back over her shoulder every few minutes. "Do I want to know what's in those?"

"I hope so," he replied, setting the shovel down.

"Who told you I was here?"

He paused. "Tommy."

"*Tommy?* Why would he tell you where I am?"

Alastair shrugged. "Because I begged. It's interestin' that ye found yerself a spot so close, though. Saves me from havin' to persuade ye to leave yer post to come with me. I get the feelin' ye'd have shot me properly if I'd asked ye to do that." He chuckled. "I wasnae sure what to expect when he said ye'd be dressed as a boy. Ye're still too pretty to trick me, mind, but it suits ye. Ye look... comfortable. Ye never used to look comfortable when ye dressed in all those petticoats and all that."

He hauled one of the sacks out of the grave and, with an anxious smile, untied a string from around the bunched mouth and opened it wide.

Fiona winced and peeked inside. A gasp slipped from her lips, her hand clamping across her mouth as she looked upon the painted, varnished bodies of nutcrackers, dolls, reindeer, Christmas doves, and perfect little hedgehogs wearing festive bows. They were not as beautifully crafted as her father's, but it did not matter; they were somehow more beautiful because of their imperfections.

"I spent all year makin' them," Alastair told her quietly. "Once I'd whittled enough in me lodgings so I couldnae move without trippin' over a nutcracker, I moved them here. See, I figured yer faither wouldnae be able to deliver presents this year, and... I ken I disappointed ye when I saw ye last, but I didnae want to disappoint the bairns who might be waitin' for Father Christmas. I didnae want them thinkin' that they'd done somethin' wrong to make him stop comin', but I kenned nay one would do it if I didnae. So, I did it. The first part, anyway. The second part is still to come. I'm here to dig up the toys, aye, but I'm also here to ask if ye'll join me as Miss Christmas."

Fiona reached into the open sack, running her fingertips over the smooth bodies, smiling as tears stung at her eyes. She tousled the blonde hair of a doll, her heart breaking and mending all at once. Indeed, she had often wondered how she might continue her father's work, but no matter what wild ideas came to her, all had been impossible. Yet, all the while, someone *had* been tinkering away, keeping her father's dream alive whilst he festered in the gaol.

"Nothing would make me happier," she said, her voice thick, "but I can't come with you. I have a duty to Georgette. I haven't lost a ward since I began this, and... I can't afford to lose one now."

Alastair smiled and put his fingers to his lips, blasting a sharp whistle through the snowy, silent night. Another figure—taller, broader, more imposing—appeared from the shadows of a nearby mausoleum. He also wore a mask and a cloak, a shovel on his shoulder.

"You found an accomplice?" Fiona whispered, struggling to swallow her fear.

"An accomplice? Och, that's nay way to speak to a fella who's practically family," a deep, warm voice replied.

Fiona's eyes bulged. "Tommy? You're supposed to be at home with Olwyn and the bairns! I left you at the kitchen table, halfway through a rousing chorus of "God Rest Ye Merry Gentlemen." I know because I was laughing on my way out."

"I didnae want to ruin the surprise," Tommy said, pulling Fiona into one of his best, bear-like hugs. "Wasnae sure if he'd muster the courage to come find ye, either, so I let it be."

Alastair shot Tommy a pointed look. "I've got courage aplenty, thank ye very much." He turned his attention back to Fiona. "Tommy has been helpin' me since the spring, when I managed to pin him down. He's nae an easy man to find when ye daenae ken where he's goin' to be."

"Of course, his first question was how ye were farin'," Tommy interjected, smirking. "I told him ye were farin' well enough."

Alastair's cheeks reddened. "I was worried, that's all. The Old Town is nay place for fine ladies, and I wasnae sure if ye and yer ma would survive it."

"They're tougher than ye think," Tommy said with a proud nod.

Fiona smiled. "I'm still surprised that *you* are still alive, Alastair. Glad, of course, but you seemed to be in a dire predicament when you came to the bridge to make sure I returned home safely."

"Ye... saw that?" Alastair swallowed loudly. "Aye, well, I found a way to save me skin. Found the address of that Mr. Walker and gave it to them, told them to ransack it, and told them when they could do it without riskin' bein' caught. They stole a hearty fortune and considered me debt paid. Am I proud of it? Aye, I am. He left yer pa rottin' in that gaol, after all yer pa had done for him. And while I couldnae help in gettin' yer pa out of the gaol, I could gain some justice for him."

"I don't know whether to applaud you or be thoroughly appalled," Fiona said with a stiff laugh, wishing she could have seen Mr. Walker's vile face when he returned to his fine townhouse to find it plundered.

Tommy shrugged. "I did both."

"We havenae given up," Alastair urged in earnest, shyly pushing his hands into the pockets of his trousers. "Tommy and I have been makin' toys, aye, but we've also been searchin' for a way to free yer pa. We made ourselves a nuisance to a few lawyers until they'd listen to us—which is easier to do when Tommy is the one demandin' to be listened to—and we raised some money. All seemed to be goin' well, but then... they let us down. Still, we're nae goin' to surrender 'til he's out in the world again as a free man—are we, Tommy?"

The bigger man shook his head. "Nae while there's still breath in me lungs."

On the verge of tears of the warmest kind, melted by the fire of their determination, Fiona walked up to the man who kept saving her, kept fighting for her even when she did not deserve it, and wrapped her arms around him. She buried her face in his shoulder, damp with snow, and held on tight.

"Oi, ye're makin' a man feel unwanted," Tommy complained, putting his giant arms around the pair of them, like the glass shell of a lantern, keeping in the glow and the warmth.

Fiona chuckled. "Thank you. Both of you. Thank you."

"It's our pleasure," Tommy replied, while Alastair just slipped his arms around Fiona in return, holding her close, his lips lightly pressed against the side of her neck.

But whether he kissed her skin or merely whispered something against it, she did not know; all she could feel was magic, restored once more on Christmas Eve. In that moment, all felt right with the world again. Better, even.

Chapter Seventeen

Despite a few nagging doubts, and a slight tremor of guilt in her belly that turned and twisted here and there, Fiona had eventually been persuaded to leave her post at Georgette's side. Tommy had offered to take up the night watch in her place, so she could walk in her father's footsteps once more, under the strict proviso that if the gifts were not all delivered by dawn, Tommy would take over whatever was left.

She could not explain why, but Fiona wanted to be with Georgette when the sun came up, perhaps so the poor girl would have some friendly company on the dawning of Christmas Day.

"Sleep well," Fiona whispered to the headstone, as she heaved one of the weighty sacks across her back. "It has ceased snowing, but the clouds are still in the sky. I think more might fall before the morning, so wrap up warm."

Tommy eyed her as if she had taken leave of her senses. "Ye ken she's dead, aye?"

"That doesn't mean she's entirely gone," Fiona replied defensively. "I've seen things, Tommy, and if her ghost is here, I want her to know someone is here, someone is treating her with kindness."

Tommy frowned, as if he had not thought of that. "What have ye seen, exactly?"

"Things I dare not speak aloud," Fiona teased, seizing her one opportunity to ruffle Tommy's thick hair. "But if you see children running around at two or three o'clock in the morning, don't immediately assume they're alive."

Tommy batted her hand away. "What did ye have to say that for? Now, I'm goin' to be jumpin' at every bloody sound!"

"At least you won't fall asleep while you're on duty." Fiona laughed and made her way to Alastair, who awaited her a short way down the hilly slope. She felt calmer already, knowing that Tommy would not waver from his guardianship of the grave, and that the remaining sacks of toys would also have someone watching over them. Indeed, even if Tommy did not care what happened to Georgette's grave, he would certainly care what happened to the gifts that he and Alastair had spent a year making.

In the foggy light of the streetlamps, they walked side-by-side, sneaking out of the cemetery and around the back of a strange structure that resembled a very tiny castle, with a jutting turret adorned with a slate spire and a mean looking spike. It was rumoured to have been Queen Mary's bath house, once upon a time, set apart from Holyrood Palace.

"Won't we get in trouble for this?" Fiona whispered, her nerves getting the better of her as they squeezed through a gap in the iron fence and found themselves on the green expanse that surrounded the palace.

Alastair waved a dismissive hand. "I do it all the time. As long as ye're nae caught, ye'll be fine."

He pressed on into the dark and she hurried to keep pace with him, the pair creeping around the back of the grand palace and the ancient ruins of a beautiful, ancient abbey that, rather respectably, had been left in its state of gothic disrepair, adjoining the rear of the palace.

Fiona closed her eyes for a moment and imagined monks singing hymns, though perhaps they had been the silent kind; she was not certain.

Nevertheless, capped with snow, torchlight dancing against the glorious archways and glassless windows that might once have been stained in all manner of vivid colours, it only added to the enchantment that seemed to be weaving through the city that night, reminding her that, even when things were not as she wanted them to be, there was beauty and wonder everywhere.

"That sack ye're carryin' has yer faither's toys in it," Alastair said suddenly, as they rounded the palace and found themselves back in the Old Town, just coming from the opposite direction to their usual method.

Fiona halted abruptly. "Pardon?"

"I found some hidden in the old workshop," he explained, shifting his sack to the other shoulder. "Under floorboards at the very back. I think yer faither must have forgotten about them, too, but I went in to see if there were any tools left behind, and I heard this... tickin' sound. I pulled up the boards and there they were—twenty or so toys. Clockwork ones, too. Managed to get a whole sack-full back from the thieves that ransacked it, an' all. They couldnae sell the toys and didnae want to give them away, so they were goin' to burn them for firewood. I followed them—actually followed them, this time—and grabbed one of the sacks from the street while they were inside. Some lad chased me for a while, but didnae see me face, and I think they were likely glad they had one less sack to worry about."

Fiona set the bag down beneath one of the streetlamps and opened up the neck, her heart aching as she lifted one of the precious toys out.

It was a little drummer boy—one of her favourites. Crouching down, she put the little drummer boy on the pavement and turned the key in his back, holding her breath. A few moments later, the drummer boy began to play, walking slowly as he beat his sticks against the drum.

Fiona watched in awe, still holding her breath, as if the drummer by might stop if she exhaled.

"Is that yers?" a small voice asked.

Fiona glanced up to find a boy observing from the stoop of a rickety house. "It belongs to Father Christmas," she said with a smile, hastily brushing tears from her cheeks. "I'm Miss Christmas. What's your name?"

The boy's eyes widened. "I'm Nathan. Do ye... really ken Faither Christmas?"

"He's my pa," Fiona replied, gesturing up at Alastair. "And this is one of his helpers. We're delivering his toys tonight, for the very best boys and girls in Edinburgh. Truth be told, I already knew your name, Nathan. You're at the top of the list for the kindest boys in the city, maybe even Scotland. But shouldn't you be in bed, fast asleep?"

Nathan chewed his lower lip, rising up off the stoop. "Ma sent me out. Told me nae to come back in 'til the shoutin' stopped." He shrugged. "Got hit with a jar of jam last week 'cause I wouldnae leave, so now I do what I'm telt. Am I really on that list?"

"I promise," Fiona said, fighting to keep her anger towards his parents out of her voice, "and that's why you get one of the very best presents. This little drummer boy is for you, Nathan."

Nathan's mouth fell open. "For me? Nay, ye're teasin' me."

"I swear. Father Christmas told me to deliver this toy to you, and only you," Fiona insisted, picking up the clockwork toy and taking it to the boy. With one hand stroking his soft, downy blonde hair, she passed him the gift. "But you have to promise to take very good care of it. When your ma tells you to come outside, you take him with you, and you play with him until it's safe to go back in. Yes?"

The boy nodded, cradling the treasure to his chest. "I willnae let anythin' happen to this, Miss Christmas. I promise ye."

"Well then, Merry Christmas, Nathan." She ruffled his hair gently, one more time, and gathered up her sack of toys. "Don't tell anyone you saw us. The magic doesn't work if you tell the secret, but we'll be back next year, and we'll come to you first.

Maybe, I might have a mince pie or a piece of figgy pudding for you, too."

The boy grinned. "I willnae tell a soul. But... can I tell me ma, else she might nae let me keep it?"

"You can tell your ma," Fiona replied.

Alastair took hold of her arm at that moment, likely knowing that she would not leave if someone did not make her, and together they continued on down the street, wielding their sacks of presents. Now and then, Fiona glanced back, her heart filling to the brim as she watched the boy playing in the light of a streetlamp, turning the key again and again to see the drummer boy play.

This is the part I never get to see, she realised, treasuring it more than she had ever treasured anything in her life. Aside from, perhaps, the last hug her father had given her. And the kiss Alastair had pressed to her hand, in the gloom of Greyfriars Kirkyard.

***

It was a Christmas Eve like no other, a gift that could not be put into words, and it seemed that Fiona was not alone in feeling like something that was lost had been given back to her. At the doors they knocked on, there was surprise and then, relief, with offers of food and drink more intense than ever before, not to be refused under any circumstances.

"We thought ye were nae comin'," one woman said. "We've been tryin' to warn the bairns for weeks, so they wouldnae be too sad."

"We heard about yer da," another said, offering profuse apologies. "We've been tryin' to put us heads together to think of a way to help, but we couldnae think of a bloody thing."

"Mrs. Donohue came around a few months back, askin' for anythin' we could spare for yer da. I couldnae give much, but… och, it gladdens me heart that ye're here. How is yer da? Has there been any news?" asked another, stunning Fiona, and when she told the woman that there had been no news, no change, they had shared a meaningful embrace. Both joyful and sorrowful, all at once.

Leaving that particular residence, Alastair made an admission. "That's how we raised some of the money for those crooked lawyers," he explained. "There's nary a soul in the Old Town that doesnae ken Mrs. Donohue, and… though it didnae work, I daenae think she has given up either."

"She told me it was hopeless," Fiona mumbled, dumbstruck by the welcome they were receiving; in awe of the generosity of people who had no need to be.

Alastair nodded. "Aye, she was sorry for that. Felt a little guilty for the way she turned ye away."

"She never needs to feel guilty." Fiona mustered a wry smile. "Even after she sent me away, I didn't listen. I knocked on a hundred other doors and heard far worse, believe me. She was being cruel to be kind; I understand that now. Sometimes, offering hope is crueller."

Alastair cast her a sideways glance. "Can I ask ye somethin'?"

"I can't stop you," she replied, grinning.

"Have ye... been well this past year?" He rubbed the back of his neck, clearly uncomfortable. "Tommy has told me things here and there, but he's sort of... silent when it comes to ye and yer ma. Said it wasnae his place to tell me about ye, and that I ought to find me nerve and speak to ye meself."

Fiona paused and took out two of the roasted chestnuts they had been given by one of the kind souls from the last tenement. She passed one to him, and bit into her own, blowing into the centre to cool it. "I've... fared better than I thought I would, not that I ever thought I'd have to experience this." She frowned. "It's strange, but if I hadn't become a nightwatchman for the dead, I think I would have been driven to the brink of madness. There's... peace in that work. It reminds you that... well, you're still breathing and as long as you are, it's not... finished. Perhaps, I *do* sound mad, but... I think I understand why Bobby watches over his master like he does. It gives him peace."

"I never did it again, by the way," Alastair said shyly. "Aside from that hole with nothin' in it but toys, I never dug into a grave again. Although, when I heard what ye were doin', there were times when I thought I might pretend, just to have ye come over and yell at me again."

Fiona smiled. "I wouldn't have merely yelled at you. How *is* your arm?"

"Just a scratch," he replied. "How's yer ma?"

Fiona's smile faded. "Lonely, I think. She is employed by this wealthy old widow, and... I think she sees more of a likeness between them than she'd care to admit. But she tries not to show it, she does her best like we all do, and even when I know she's been sobbing through the night, she gets up in the morning, she puts on a brave smile, and she carries on." She paused. "When I tell her about your and Tommy's efforts, and how the people here rallied together for papa, I think it'll please her. It won't fix it, but it'll... ache less for a while, maybe."

Finishing their chestnuts, they walked on for a while, to reach the top of their next street.

"So, ye never did marry that "good man from a good family" then?" Alastair asked, a few paces from the next door.

Fiona had to laugh. "No, as it turned out, the notion of having their son married to a thief's daughter did not align with their picture of the future. The note they sent was quite something. It even said, "Please, do not respond." I should have kept it to amuse me on difficult days, but I think we burned it in the fireplace on the first night we came to Canongate."

"Wasnae worthy of ye anyway," Alastair mumbled.

Fiona weaved her arm through his, pulling him against her side. "You never did tell me what you were going to say that night in the kirkyard—the thing both of us might regret."

"I cannae remember sayin' that," he replied, a note too quickly. "Was probably somethin' rude that would've offended yer dainty ears."

Fiona chuckled. "Very well, don't tell me."

"I cannae remember!" he insisted, though the redness of his cheeks and the mischievous glint in his eyes, and the way he pulled her closer said otherwise. "Speakin' of things nay one is sayin', I'm surprised more of the folk here havenae mentioned ye're wearin' trousers."

Fiona shrugged. "Let's be honest, it's probably not even close to the strangest thing they've seen in these streets."

"Aye, ye've a point there." He raised his fist and knocked on the next door, his arm still looped through hers, keeping her tight to his side.

Chapter Eighteen

Across the city, church bells tolled five chimes, though dawn would not rise for hours yet. And as the last chime sounded, it was accompanied by the gentle slam of the last door, Fiona and Alastair's last toy handed out, ready for the wide-eyed gratitude of a waking child.

"Another successful year," Alastair said, draping the empty sack around his neck like a scarf.

Fiona nodded. "All thanks to you and Tommy."

"Nay, all thanks to yer da." Alastair swept his hand in a half-circle. "He started all of this, and he'll return to it one day. I ken ye said that offerin' hope is crueller sometimes, but... it's Christmas Day. On Christmas Day, ye wish for miracles, and I'm nae sayin' anyone is listenin', but ye've been loiterin' in kirkyards for so long that I reckon ye've a closer correspondence with the heavens than most."

Fiona sighed, covering up a yawn. "Speaking of which, I ought to be getting back to Georgette. I'm sure she was thrilled with Tommy's company, but I want to describe the sunrise to her."

They had been back and forth to Calton Cemetery a few times during the night to fetch fresh toys from the unusual cache, and though Tommy had kept to his promise to perform her duties, he had been looking a little weary the last time they went back. Bored, in truth.

"Can I come with ye?" Alastair asked. "I have to gather up the sacks for next year anyway, and someone should fill in the grave so nay one thinks there's been a snatchin', but... I could linger for a while, if ye wouldnae mind some company?"

Fiona held out her hand. "I'd like that."

"Onward, then." He took her hand and squeezed it gently, his rough palm warm against hers, despite the cold morning.

Making their way up the Royal Mile, they soon came to the top of Cockburn Street, where Fiona halted and took a moment to catch her breath. Her heart raced and her lungs tightened, making every inhale feel as if she was trying to draw air through stone.

"I always avoid this spot," she confessed, gripping Alastair's hand tighter, to ground herself. "I just... can't look at it."

Alastair smiled down at her. "I'm here, lass. I'll hold ye steady, but if ye cannae do it, we can walk the other way. It'll take longer, aye, but I'm in nay hurry."

"No, this way," she choked, pulling him forward.

The cobblestones of Cockburn Street glittered with a thin capelet of snow, slippery underfoot, as if they had known she might need something to distract herself—namely, staying upright.

Alastair held her tightly as they stumbled and staggered down the steep slope, past the opening of the passageway to Jackson's Close.

Fiona glanced at it, her heart sore, but soon, she was past it and her chest began to loosen, her heart slowing. It was just a workshop. It was just a place.

The real magic had belonged to a person, not stone and mortar, and that spell that her father had weaved still enchanted the streets and the people therein. She had seen it with her own eyes that night; the power of her father's kindness, even in his absence.

Continuing to retrace familiar steps, the pair soon found themselves in the shadow of the park, scrambling down the slope to the paths below. And though it was not even close to dawn, the gardens were awake, the scent of roasted chestnuts and hot cider swirling on the wind.

"Wait here," Alastair said, running off.

Fiona stared into the darkness he had vanished into, her mouth open in protest, though no sound came out. Instead, her eyes squinted into the gloom, making out the shapes of drunkards and beggars on the benches opposite. She watched for the rise and fall of sunken chests, strangely soothed by the rattling sound of snores.

A short while later, footsteps approached at a clip. Alastair appeared, grinning like a boy, clutching a brown paper bag in one hand and two tin cups in the other. "Breakfast," he declared, passing one cup to her. "I told Ginny I'd bring the cups back later."

"Ginny?" Fiona's heart plummeted.

"Aye. Kenned her since I was knee-high. I used to steal from her cart, so she'd just give me bits of whatever she was sellin' in the end." He laughed, shifting the paper bag into his cup-holding hand so he could take hold of Fiona's hand again. It was hot from cradling the mulled cider. "When it's winter, she sells the best cider."

Fiona took a breath. "So, not a secret wife?"

"She's about three times me age!" He laughed, and Fiona's cheeks promptly flooded with embarrassment. "And nay, I havenae got a secret wife. How could I, when I've been pinin' for someone else since I was three-and-ten?"

Fiona blinked. "Pardon?"

"Och, fell in love with her the moment I took her hand," he said, hiding a smile behind the rim of his cider cup. "Hopeless, really. I was just an urchin, nae worthy of her, and then I heard she was gettin' married to some high-and-mighty lad. Broke me heart, to be fair. Always wondered what happened to her. Someone told me she'd taken to dressin' up like a boy, sittin' by headstones like a tortured poet, so maybe she's been pinin' for me too, waitin' for me to come by with me shovel to dig up some poor soul for anatomists who ought to ken better."

Fiona swallowed thickly, her heart beating so hard she feared he could hear it. "Alastair, I—"

"Tommy will have me neck if we daenae get back soon," he interrupted hastily, as if terrified of what she was about to say. "We can drink this and eat them chestnuts when we get to Georgette. Share some with her, maybe, though I daenae ken how that would work."

He tugged her along, pressing on through the darkness as the city began to awaken, for even on Christmas Day, there were countless men and women and children who did not have the luxury of staying at home with their families.

Work needed to be done, money needed to be made, and though employers could choose to be generous, not all were conscious of treating their workers like actual people who might enjoy a day of concentrating on nothing but what truly mattered: family, love, and peace.

Yet, the entire way to Calton Cemetery, Fiona's mind whipped and whirled like a winter storm, overwhelmed by Alastair's words.

There could be no denying what he had been trying to say, nor that he had been baring his soul to her, so why had he not allowed her to reply? And why could she *not* reply, even now, walking in companionable silence with him along the New Town streets she had once known so well?

I have loved you since that day, too. She knew it with every fibre of her being, but the words would not rise up. Her tongue locked whenever she tried, and judging by the sad shine in Alastair's eyes, he was fast losing hope of her reciprocating.

"There ye are!" Tommy grumbled, as the pair lumbered up the hill towards him. "I heard them bells chimin' five, and realised I'm gettin' too old to be sittin' out in the cold. I cannae feel me knees. I ken that sounds strange, but... och, ye'll understand when ye're an ancient auld goat like me." He eyed the two of them. "What's wrong with ye? Did ye have some trouble?"

Fiona shook her head. "Everything went... perfectly. The sacks are empty, and bairns will be waking up to gifts, as always."

"Ye're thinkin' about yer da?" Tommy pulled an apologetic face. "And here I am, whinin' about me knees."

Fiona shrugged. "I think he knows. I think he'll feel it, wherever he is."

"Well, the lass didnae stir and I didnae see any of them ghosts and ghouls ye were teasin' me about," Tommy said brightly, though it echoed hollow. "There was a fella a few hours ago, prowlin' around, but... I think he was real. Och, ye've got me doubtin' me own eyes!"

Fiona mustered a laugh. "Thank you for taking care of her."

"Thank ye for nae beltin' me for nae tellin' ye about all of this sooner," Tommy replied, sweeping Fiona up into a warm hug, as if she was as much his own daughter as she was Donal's. "Now," he said, setting her down on her feet, "if ye daenae mind, I'm goin' to find some breakfast, then I'll come back, and we can all return to Canongate together. Olwyn told me I was to bring ye, since yer ma will be at that old lady's house."

Fiona gawped at him. "Olwyn knew?"

"Aye, course she did." Tommy chuckled. "I nearly spilled the secret a few weeks back, when ye were playin' with the bairns. I've never seen her so angry at me!"

Fiona smacked him lightly on the arm. "You're all wretched! Delightfully, wonderfully wretched, but wretched nonetheless!" She smacked Alastair too, for good measure. "But... thank you. A thousand times, thank you. I think that might've been the best Christmas Eve yet, and when my father comes home, and he *will* come home, then it'll be perfection."

"Did ye wish for it?" Alastair said softly.

Fiona smiled. "I can't say, or it might not come true."

"Right, now that I've had me beltin', I'll be off," Tommy announced, handing back the pepper-box pistol to Fiona. "Daenae shoot Alastair again while I'm gone. He's nae a bad lad, really." He flashed a wink at Alastair and headed off down the hill, whistling a carol as he went.

And whether it was the music of his pursed lips, conjuring a spell, or whether it was just the heavens unburdening themselves, Fiona did not know, but as the whistle carried on the breeze, fresh snowflakes began to fall.

***

"That warms the soul, doesn't it?" Fiona cradled the still-warm cup of cider as she sat beside Alastair beneath the makeshift lean-to, next to Georgette's resting place.

He took a satisfying sip. "The snow or the cider? Or the fact that there's bairns wakin' up to toys this mornin'?"

"Both. All of it." She puffed out a happy sigh, a thought sliding into her mind. "Actually, there's something I've been meaning to give you. I would've given it to you sooner, but... well, I couldn't find you. I didn't know if you were alive or dead, so I... just held onto it. I think it might have been a lucky charm for me and my ma, but it belongs to you. You should have it back."

Alastair raised a curious eyebrow. "What is it?"

Slowly, she reached into the pocket of her coat and pulled out the precious treasure, in all its crooked, ugly, beautiful glory. She had worn a patch of the hedgehog's snout smooth with anxious rubbing over the past year, taking comfort from the smooth feel of it beneath her thumb. "You left it on that headstone. I didn't want him to get cold, so I put him in my pocket. He's been in a variety of pockets ever since, always close to me."

Alastair's eyes widened, a gasp crackling out of his lips. "I thought... I'd lost it. I went back for it, but it was gone. So were me tools, so I figured someone just snatched it all." He paused. "Ye didnae take me tools too, did ye?"

"Just the hedgehog." She put the misshapen creature into the palm of his hand and folded his fingers over the top of it. "It has been my honour to look after him."

His knuckles whitened as he clutched the hedgehog. "Thank ye," he murmured. "Thank ye for keepin' him safe."

"I'm sorry for how we parted ways," she went on, nervous. "I'm sorry you got hurt because of me. I'm sorry I didn't tell you that I was to be betrothed, though... I never wanted to be. I knew it would help my family, so I didn't argue, but even if I had married him, my heart would never have been his. You see, a thief stole it a long time ago."

Alastair froze, his body stiffening.

"I was twelve, running for my life down a passageway, and he caught hold of my hand and pulled me to safety," she continued, her voice trembling. "He helped me to finish my father's work, and with every step we took around those streets, knocking on doors, giving out toys, I fell in love with him. But he vanished into thin air that night, and for four years I thought I'd imagined him. I think everyone else thought I'd imagined him too, until he literally burst back into my life, knocking into me so hard that I had bruises for weeks.

"I thought that would be the last I saw of him, until I rescued him from a constable's clutches. He was older, then. Handsome. And I made him help deliver the toys before I'd give back this sack of things he'd stolen." She paused, breathless. "Tommy knew before I knew, that I was in danger of being helplessly in love with this boy. And when he kissed my hand in Greyfriars Kirkyard, I knew I was doomed. I knew I would love him forever, even if I never saw him again, and there was a good chance of that, because there were some men who wanted him dead. I often wonder what happened to him."

Alastair turned to face her, his breath steaming in the snowy air. His eyes gleamed with a curious sort of pain, as he lifted his hand to her face, his thumb gently stroking the rosy apple of her cheek. "I daenae ken him meself, but I reckon a day never went by that he didnae think of ye," he whispered, smiling. "I reckon he kept himself alive, just in case ye crossed paths again."

"If only he would find me, I would tell him how dearly I love him," Fiona whispered back, her heart turning somersaults. "I would tell him that *he* is a good man. The best of men."

In the distance, atop the rocky mound where the castle watched over the city, a piper began to play as the snow danced around their shelter. The fine hairs prickled up the back of Fiona's neck, that sound so ancient and stirring that tears welled in her eyes. And as she closed them, a tear escaped, spilling down her cheek and rushing to meet the soft press of Alastair's lips on hers.

She heard the faint rustle of him setting down his cup, before she felt his arms wrap tightly around her, pulling her into the warmth of him. Her own arms looped around his neck as he kissed her more deeply, and she kissed him back with all the love that her broken heart had to give.

"I love ye," he whispered against her lips, cupping her face. "I love ye. Thank ye, love."

"For what?" she mumbled in reply, dazed by joy.

He smiled. "For nae marryin' a rich man."

Laughing softly, she kissed him again, and as the piper played and the snow fell and the city stirred to the beauty of Christmas Day, Fiona knew that this was a gift that would last a lifetime.

Chapter Nineteen

Dawn had finally broken, casting a stormy light across Edinburgh as the snow clouds continued their slow scud across the sky, and though Alastair had fallen asleep, his head upon Fiona's lap, she had not wavered from her duty, feeding the feeble fire that Tommy had built during his part of the watch as she spoke to Georgette. Someone from Georgette's household would be arriving soon, to pay her for her first watch, but until they came, she could not leave. Would not leave.

"It's going to be a pretty one," she told Georgette in a hushed whisper, so as not to wake Alastair. "There's thick snow on the ground, the piper is still playing, and your visitors will soon be here. I hope they sit with you for a while, and I imagine I'll see you again tonight. Hopefully, I'll have some new stories to tell."

Just then, on the path at the bottom of the slope, a carriage trundled up from the main road. It pulled to a slow halt, the horses skittish. It was an elegant carriage—expensive—letting Fiona know that it was not a servant of the household who had been sent to pay her.

Hurriedly, she poked Alastair in the side. He opened his bleary eyes, smiling up at her, but as his hand sought her cheek, she took hold of it and shook her head. "Georgette's family are here. Sit up and pretend you're just… an associate."

His eyes widened and he did as she had asked, smacking his cheeks lightly as he stifled a yawn and stretched from side to side, before sitting straight-backed as if he had just been scolded by a schoolmaster.

Two figures descended from the carriage—a handsome gentleman of forty or so, and a beautiful lady of similar age, dressed in a mournful gown of black bombazine, a gauzy dark veil shrouding her face. The man held the woman tightly, as though he was the only thing keeping her upright, making their funereal way up the slope to the grave.

Fiona's heart ached for them, noting how pale and drawn the lady looked beneath the thin veil, as if the loss of Georgette had sapped the life out of her too. Yet, there was something about the woman that gave Fiona pause. She looked… familiar, somehow. A resemblance that Fiona could not quite pinpoint.

As the grief-stricken couple neared, Fiona got to her feet and bowed her head, cursing inwardly as she noted her cloth cap on the ground.

Her hair had tumbled free, and once they saw that she was not the boy she claimed to be, perhaps they would dispense with her services. Yet, to reach for the cap and jam it on her head seemed fruitless, for they were too close not to notice.

Just then, a wrenching wail pierced the air.

Fiona peered up at the couple, hesitating as she saw the woman crumble, not knowing whether to offer assistance or not. The woman had dropped to her knees, and though the husband pulled urgently on her arm, she would not move. Instead, she pointed a shaking finger straight at Fiona, staring right at her as tears streamed down her face, howling the same thing over and over, "Georgette! It is Georgette!"

The husband glanced at Fiona... and staggered back, letting go of his wife's arm as shock rippled across his face. He shook his head, squinting at Fiona, rubbing his eyes as if he could not believe them. "Georgette?" he asked, his voice quivering.

"Me?" Fiona pointed at herself, utterly bewildered. "No, I am not Georgette. I am... the one you employed to watch over her last night."

The man frowned. "But, you are not a boy."

"No, but I am very good at my work," Fiona insisted, feeling her reputation slipping away. If these people told anyone, she would struggle to be hired again. "My name is Fiona, but I tell my employers that I am a boy so they will not worry for my welfare. But I really am good at my work."

The man lifted his wife to her feet, putting his arm around her waist, heaving her towards Fiona and Georgette.

But coming closer only made the poor woman weep harder, her entire body shaking.

And when there were only a few paces left between the couple and Fiona, the woman lurched forward, reaching for Fiona. Fiona caught her, holding her, whilst staring desperately over her shoulder at the husband.

"I have taken good care of her," Fiona promised, gently stroking the woman's hair. "I spoke to her all night, so she wouldn't feel alone."

"Oh, my Georgette," the woman sobbed, gripping Fiona so tight that her ribs began to ache. "You came back. It is a miracle. You came back."

Fiona frowned. "I'm not Georgette, Ma'am."

At that moment, the husband stepped forward to reclaim his wife, pulling her into his chest as she wept and called for the daughter she had lost. But as he embraced her and tried his best to soothe her, he eyed Fiona closely, his brow furrowing as a small, confused noise cracked in the back of his throat.

"I must apologize for my wife," he said, at length, his voice unsteady with feeling. "But, you see, you look so very much like our darling Georgette. What did you say your name was?"

"Fiona. Fiona McVey." She hesitated. "Please, don't dispense with me because I lied about being a boy. I never waver in my duties. I have never lost one of my wards, in all the time I have been doing this. I—"

"McVey?" The wife turned slowly in her husband's arms, her eyes wide as if she really was looking at a ghost. "Is your mother named Beryl? Is her maiden name Bastion?"

Fiona flinched. "Yes."

"And your father is Donal McVey?" The woman sounded like she was about to choke.

Fiona felt as though the world was spinning faster, the ground turning into liquid, her legs shaky. "Do you… know them?"

The woman crumbled again, sinking down to her knees on the snow-coated ground, one hand clawing at her husband's coat.

A guttural groan keened from her trembling lips, stirring up the ghosts that haunted the cemetery. Fiona could feel them watching, the hairs standing up on the back of her neck.

Perhaps, they thought someone had come to visit them. Perhaps, it was Georgette, wishing she could offer comfort to her mother.

"Come… to me," the woman urged.

Hesitantly, Fiona obeyed, crouching down in front of the poor creature. "How do you know my parents?" she whispered, taking hold of the lady's free hand. "I feel like… I should know you."

"Beryl," the woman whimpered. "My Beryl. My Georgette."

Fiona held the woman's hand tighter. "You know my mother?"

"My sister," the lady gasped, tugging her husband's coat so vehemently that a button popped. "My Beryl. I have… missed her. My sister."

Fiona looked up at the husband for explanation, whilst Alastair hung back, clearly realising that something bizarre was afoot.

"Harriet," he said softly, kneeling beside his wife. "You must rally yourself. I cannot explain this for you. I do not know what you know, only what you have told me."

But the broken creature could not speak, overcome with a misery that Fiona could not fathom. It was as if she were possessed by grief itself; a monstrous thing that stole words and joy, and twisted them into plangent sounds that brought tears to the eyes of strangers.

"Her sister... was shunned from the family some twenty years ago," the man said uncertainly. "I met her several times, for I was already married to my darling Harriet here. I was there when she was cast out. She... fell in love with... goodness, what was he?"

"A clock... maker's... assistant," Harriet found some semblance of her voice, croaking out the details.

The man nodded. "Yes, a clockmaker's assistant. She was betrothed to a baronet, I think, at the time. An Englishman." He pursed his lips. "I believe she went to a shop to have her father's pocket-watch repaired as a gift, and that is where she met... that man."

"My... father?" Fiona blinked, hearing the words but not quite absorbing them.

"If your mother is—or was—Beryl Bastion, then yes. I would assume that man was your father. Mr. McVey." The man cleared his throat and offered his hand. "I am George Arbroath, and this is my wife, Harriet. Thank you for... taking care of our daughter."

Harriet shook her head. "She *is* our daughter. Look at her!"

"I know, my darling, but she is not our daughter," George replied apologetically. "I believe she might be... your niece. Our niece. Georgette's cousin. It would... explain the likeness."

A tear crept down his cheek, and he could not look at Fiona for long, likely too painful to see an echo of the child he had lost.

Harriet shuffled towards Fiona on her knees, putting her hands on Fiona's shoulders and staring hard into the younger woman's eyes. "My sister is... your mother?"

"I do not know, Ma'am. I can't make sense of this," Fiona said quietly. "But... you were familiar to me, when I saw you approach. Might you... lift your veil for a moment?"

With shaky hands, Harriet obliged... and Fiona knew immediately that they were not mistaken.

Harriet was a slightly older version of her mother, with fairer hair, her eyes perhaps greener than Beryl's, her face maybe rounder, but there could be no denying that they shared the same blood, the same family. Indeed, Fiona could see her own face reflected in the older woman's, for she had always been her mother's twin.

Sometimes, her father had joked that Fiona was glad that she was "all Beryl's," claiming she would have been an ugly thing if she had resembled him.

"My mother used to tell me she had a sister," Fiona said, remembering the tales her mother would whisper at night, when Fiona was a child, describing grand parties and fantastical balls. There had always been a sister in those stories, and now that Fiona thought of it, the sister had disappeared from those tales as Fiona grew older, and began to ask questions. Her mother would say she was tired and end the story there.

Harriet lightly stroked Fiona's cheeks, wrapping a coil of hair gently around her forefinger. "You look so like her. My Georgette. My Beryl." Her breath hitched. "I never... dared to search for her, but... I wanted to. I have... missed her. My Georgette... found you... for me. George, I think our... daughter found her for me."

"It is a curious coincidence," George replied, dabbing his cheeks with his handkerchief. His grief was quieter, but no less potent.

"Is my sister... alive?" Harriet pleaded.

Fiona gave a small nod. "She is. She will be at Mrs. Ogilvy's house, at present."

"Mrs. Ogilvy?" Harriet looked startled.

"You know her?"

It seemed as if Harriet might faint, swaying slightly. "She was... a dear friend of my grandmother. She adored us girls, treating us as if we were her own granddaughters." She touched her palm to her forehead, like she was trying to hold in the tide of her thoughts. "She offered sanctuary to my sister after... Beryl broke the engagement with that awful baronet. But my grandmother threatened to never see Mrs. Ogilvy again if she did so. I still think she would have taken Beryl in, but... Beryl could not face ruining a lifelong friendship. So, Beryl left the house and never came back."

That *is why she treats us with such kindness,* Fiona realised, thinking of all the food that Mrs. Ogilvy sent Beryl home with, and the invitations to take tea with her. Fiona had known that was peculiar, but now it made perfect sense.

"We must fetch her!" Harriet shrieked, turning to her husband. "We must fetch Beryl. You must both come to dinner."

George nodded. "Of course, you must come to dine with us. We are having a simple Christmas feast, but... it will be a comfort to have my wife's sister restored to her. I think it... will be of help." His gaze flitted to the headstone. "I think this is what Georgette would have wanted."

"Georgette has done this," Harriet agreed, lumbering to her feet. "My darling Georgette, always... thinking of me."

She shambled to the grave and kneeled before it, pressing her fingertips to her lips before resting the ghost of that kiss on the frozen soil. George went to join her, his arm around his wife's shoulders, the distraught parents sharing a private moment with their lost daughter.

Fiona took that as her cue to move away, wandering over to the iron mortsafe of the false grave. She perched on the uncomfortable grille, smiling distractedly as Alastair sat down beside her.

"Seems me hedgehog is still bringin' ye luck," he said, taking hold of her hand and bringing it to his lips. "Or there really is somethin' to be said for folk livin' on, in a way, after they're buried in the earth."

Fiona expelled a strained breath. "I knew she was special," she mumbled. "I knew when I spoke to her that... there was something between us."

"She didnae talk back, did she?" he teased.

She shook her head. "No, but it felt like she was listening." She cast him a sideways glance. "I'm not mad, so don't send me off to an asylum."

"I wouldnae dare," he told her, kissing her hand once more.

"Do you mind if I go to this Christmas feast?"

He laughed. "Why would I mind? Just bring me somethin' delicious and tell me everythin' when I see ye tonight." He paused. "I will be seein' ye tonight, will I nae? After all, there are two sacks left that need deliverin'."

"There are?" She frowned.

"Greyfriars Kirk," he told her. "Two sacks for the church, and a head scratch for Bobby."

Fiona managed a smile. "I wouldn't miss it."

"I hoped ye'd say that."

Chapter Twenty

"This is madness," Beryl murmured, standing in front of a looking glass in a strange bedchamber in a fine townhouse in the New Town, barely two streets away from Mrs. Ogilvy's residence. She wore a pretty lavender tea dress, her hair washed and pinned, her skin scrubbed clean, though her eyes were shot through with red from the cascade of tears she had shed already, and would likely continue to shed.

Fiona, also washed, primped, and dressed in the sort of garments she had assumed she would never wear again, rested her head on her mother's shoulder, gazing at their reflection in the mirror. "You were so close to one another, all this time."

"Don't," Beryl urged, laughing awkwardly, "or I shall begin to weep again, and I fear I will not be able to stop. Your father always told me that Christmas miracles were real, but I never believed him. Now, I am beginning to suspect that he was right."

Fiona peered up at her mother. "Are you angry?"

"Angry?" Beryl canted her head. "Why would I be angry?"

"She didn't come to find you."

Beryl smiled a sad smile. "You weren't raised in the sort of household where we were raised. You were raised with love instead of fear. If you had experienced it, you would understand why she was not courageous enough to find me, and why I, in turn, didn't try to see her again, though I longed to." She hesitated. "My father, your grandfather, was not a nice man. When he found out about your father and I, and I refused to give your father up, I was certain he would kill me to spare his honour. I managed to escape, but had I returned, he truly might have killed me."

"I'm sorry." Fiona tried to imagine what her mother's childhood must have been like, but she could not, for all she had ever known was warmth and kindness.

Beryl hugged her. "You don't have to be sorry. I gained my freedom and my happiness; I only wish it had not been so many years since I last saw my sister." She stroked her daughter's hair. "Indeed, *I'm* sorry I was not honest. I'm sorry I did not tell you how I knew Mrs. Ogilvy. You see, thinking of the past has always been painful for me, and, selfishly, I didn't want to feel that pain again."

"I think I understand," Fiona said, frowning at her reflection. "Should I wear a veil or something over my face? I feel awful for Harriet. Every time she looks at me, she bursts into tears again. She was their only daughter, and I feel like I'm... being cruel just by being here."

Beryl shook her head. "It might sound peculiar, but I think it helps. I think all of this helps." She sighed. "She believes that

Georgette reunited us, and that can only be a balm for her grief."

"I wish I had met her," Fiona confessed. "I think we might have been fond of one another."

Beryl smiled, fresh tears beading. "I think so, too." From somewhere far below the bedchambers, a gong sounded. Beryl straightened up, smoothing a hand across her hair, and seized hold of her daughter's hand. "I think we are being summoned to dinner."

Descending the sweeping stairwell with hesitant steps, for both had grown unaccustomed to expensive garments and countless layers of petticoats and crinoline, Fiona's eyes widened in delight as she set her gaze, once more, on the enormous Christmas tree that stood in the entrance hall. The tiny candles had been lit, bringing twinkling starlight into the townhouse.

But it was the sight of Harriet, waiting at the bottom of the stairs, that gladdened her heart the most. Suddenly, her mother broke away from her and hurried down the rest of the steps, falling into Harriet's arms.

Harriet, in turn, clung onto Beryl as if worried she might vanish if she was not squeezed hard enough. They had been hugging like that since the moment they had been reunited in Mrs. Ogilvy's foyer, and every time they saw one another afresh, that impulse to run and embrace one another overwhelmed them once again.

It was the most beautiful thing that Fiona had ever witnessed: two sisters, reunited, their love for each other unwavering though they had been separated for years.

"How is it possible that you have become more beautiful?" Harriet crowed. "You are supposed to wither with age, not improve."

Beryl chuckled. "Then, how is it possible that *you* are more beautiful?"

"Fiona, come!" Harriet urged, her expression still flinching slightly when she looked at her niece. "Let me hold you."

Fiona made her way to the bottom of the stairs, and duly embraced her newfound aunt.

She knew that Harriet still saw Georgette and not her, and she knew that when Harriet embraced her, she was imagining her daughter, but if it soothed the older woman's grief in some small way, Fiona was happy to be a substitute.

***

With full bellies and healing hearts, the Arbroaths and the McVeys sat around the dining table while Mrs. Ogilvy—a late guest to the festivities—played the pianoforte.

Both families were missing someone, their absence bringing a quiet contemplation to the end of the feast. An empty chair had been left for Georgette, and though there was no chair for Donal, Fiona pictured him sitting beside her, making jokes and toasts, perfectly comfortable in the company of such fine people.

"So, this is all yours now?" Beryl said, swirling a glass of brandy.

Harriet nodded, looking somewhat sheepish. "I was as surprised as you. I felt certain that Father would leave it to some distant second cousin. Any male still living. But no—I inherited it all."

"How did he die?" Beryl sniffed, staring down into the amber liquid.

"He was overseeing the building of a new railway bridge," Harriet replied. "Part of it collapsed, and he was in the wrong place at the wrong moment. It was quite the funeral, as you can imagine. I wanted you to be there, but Mama refused. She was already beginning to take leave of her senses, but the worst of it began after Father passed. She is in a private asylum now. We visit occasionally, but she does not know us anymore. She speaks of you, sometimes, though. She asks for you, though I do not know if she would know you if you saw her."

Beryl took a hearty sip of her brandy. "I'm sorry I wasn't there. I'm sorry I stayed away." Her voice caught in her throat. "I have missed so much. I never got to meet my niece. Goodness, I shall regret that for the rest of my days."

"*I* am sorry," Harriet sobbed in reply, reaching across the table for Beryl's hand. "*I* have missed so much. When Father passed, I should have found you. I should have... reunited us. I am the older sister; it was my duty to do that, and to think of all you have suffered, whilst I was here, sitting upon an inheritance. I am sickened by myself!"

Beryl shook her head. "You mustn't be. We were both afraid."

The two women promptly began weeping, speaking in an incoherent dialect of misery that no one else could understand, but as they were nodding and making noises of agreement, it seemed that they understood one another perfectly.

"It goes without saying that we will do all we can and use all the influence we possess to free your father," George said, turning to Fiona, though he looked right through her. "It is a charitable thing that he has done, all these years, and I cannot abide the thought of him being imprisoned for a crime he did not commit."

Beryl had informed him of her husband's situation, earlier on in the feasting, explaining the toymaking and the deliveries that he made on Christmas Eve.

Though, it was Fiona who explained what had truly happened to the clockmaker's shop, and how her father had been framed for the crime. There were parts of the story that even Beryl did not know, pertaining to Alastair's part in the events, though Fiona did not mention him by name; she did not want her mother to blame him for what happened to her father, despite there being no cause to blame him.

Of course, neither Fiona nor her mother had expected anything to come from the revelations about Donal's fate, but Fiona *had* hoped that her newfound family might be able to do something. After all, wealth had power, and the Arbroaths were wealthier than most. Certainly, wealthier than Mr. Walker.

"You would do that for us?" Fiona said shyly.

George smiled and patted her on the arm. "You are our family, Fiona. Family protects one another. At least, this one does." He leaned closer. "I did not like your grandfather much, either. He was a terrifying man. I almost lost my nerve when I came to ask for Harriet's hand in marriage, so I must applaud the bravery of your own father, to challenge such a man for your mother's hand."

"I think eloping made it less of a challenge," Fiona replied, chuckling.

George's face pinched. "Goodness, you look so like her when you laugh." He shook his head. "I am sorry. I know it is unfair to you, for you cannot change the way you look, but… please be patient with us. The wound is still fresh, and… you are the twin of her."

"I don't mind it," Fiona admitted. "I know how painful it must be. But, if I may, I would like to continue watching over her until she is… out of danger. I liked being near to her, even when I did not know who she was. Please, allow me to keep her company."

It was at that moment that Fiona realised the other end of the table had fallen silent.

"We cannot allow you to do that," Harriet insisted, mopping her eyes with a serviette. "No, no, that would not be proper. I am grateful, of course, that you were the one watching over her, but… things have changed. You do not have to work now. We shall take care of you. Both of you."

Fiona cleared her throat. "Nevertheless, I would like to stay at my post. I do not want any payment. I just want to keep her company; I want to keep talking to her even though she will not reply. It sounds unusual, I know, but… that is my wish. My Christmas wish." She shrugged. "It is the least that I can do, considering you have promised to help my father."

"Let her," Beryl said softly, stroking her sister's hand. "Let her do this."

Harriet and George stared at one another, holding a silent conversation across the remains of roast goose, buttered potatoes, fresh bread rolls, and honeyed carrots. Harriet looked like she might cry again, and George gave a shy little nod, before announcing, "It would be our honour to have you watch her, Fiona." His voice hitched. "I think she... would appreciate your company greatly, and I know it... would soothe my heart to remember that she is not... alone or with a stranger on Christmas Day. Thank you, Fiona. Thank you."

"But you must return here in the morning," Harriet urged, her chest wracked with sobs she could not control. "You must promise."

Fiona bowed her head. "I promise."

"And *you* must stay here with me," Harriet added, gripping Beryl's hand.

Beryl nodded. "I will, sweet sister."

And though it was warm and safe inside the townhouse, surrounded by family old and new, she felt as if she had overstayed her welcome for now. Her mother and aunt had a lot to discuss, and Fiona thought it might be best if her very presence did not cause further upset to a grieving mother and father. Besides, there was one person Fiona wanted to see before Christmas Day came to a close. Even if she could not help him take the last presents to Greyfriars, she wanted to hold him and thank him, hoping that, one day, he might also be seated at this table as part of the family.

Chapter Twenty-One

Sent off with a waxed paper parcel of cold cuts, some mince pies, half a figgy pudding, and a reticule stuffed with bread rolls and a pat of butter, with a knife for spreading, Fiona wondered how bizarre she looked now that she was back in her trousers and jacket, with a beaded reticule dangling from the crook of her elbow.

She relished the cold evening air, her heart pounding faster as she reached the gates of Calton Cemetery and ran along the pathways until she came to the spot where the carriage had halted only that morning.

Her aunt and uncle had tried to insist upon her taking the carriage there, but she had insisted on walking.

She was glad that she had, the warmth of her exertions better than any coat.

Clambering up the slope, a smile was already etched upon her lips, long before she saw Alastair standing there. As if she had known he would be waiting.

What she had not anticipated were the sea of votives he had ignited all around the grave of Georgette Arbroath, nor the bunch of heather that he held shyly in his hands, like he did not quite know what to do with the purpled bouquet.

"Merry Christmas," he said, as she weaved through the votives and threw herself into his open arms.

"Merry Christmas," she whispered back, burying her face in his neck. "I brought something delicious for you."

He chuckled. "I know, I'm holdin' it."

"You're a mischievous one, Alastair…" She paused. "It occurs to me that I've kissed you, but I don't even know your surname."

"Barron," he said, smiling against her hair.

She pulled back. "You're a baron?"

"Two Rs." He grinned, arching an eyebrow. "But if that's nae good, I suppose I can just keep to meself what I was goin' to say to ye—ask ye, in truth."

She slipped her fingers into the hair at the nape of his neck, laughing breathily. "On the contrary, if you *were* a baron, I'd have to part ways with you. I don't want a man who's rich in wealth, as long as they're rich in character and love."

"Well then, do ye think ye might consent to be Mrs. Barron, and make me Christmas wish—a wish I've made since the moment I met ye—come true?" he asked bashfully. "I daenae have a ring for ye, but I have a promise. A promise to love ye and cherish ye, from this day to our last. I suppose that's why I'm askin' ye in a kirkyard." A nervy sound rumbled in his throat, struggling to hold her gaze.

Fiona beamed from ear to ear, cradling his face in her hands. Rising up on tiptoe, she pressed a chilly kiss to his lips.

"Does that mean ye will, or are ye tryin' to let me down gently?" he murmured, his eyes closed when she pulled back again.

She laughed. "With all my heart, I will. Nothing would make me happier than to spend the rest of my days with you, as your wife."

"Aye?" His eyes shot wide.

She nodded. "Aye."

He scooped her up in his arms and swung her around, whooping and howling like a merry hound, his mirth more wonderful than any carol or piper's song, purer than any fresh fallen snow.

She howled with him, laughing like a madwoman as the twirl of their bodies swayed the flames of the votives, revelling in the happiness of the moment.

Gradually, they slowed, and he set her down on the ground, bending his head to kiss her. The touch of his lips brimmed with anxiety and joy in equal measure, and she kissed him back in kind, overwhelmed by the merriment in her heart.

Indeed, she did not know if she had ever felt so happy in all her life, for he had found her, her mother had found a lost sister, and with any luck, it would not be long before her father returned to her, to claim back the mantle that Alastair had borrowed for a while, restoring the pieces of Christmas that had been missing, plus those that Fiona had not known were missing.

"I love you," she said, pressing her palms to his chest to feel his heart beating.

"I love ye more," he insisted, kissing her again.

Pausing in their kiss, Fiona sighed. "We should make our way to Greyfriars before the hour gets too late. I have some goose for Bobby."

"Tommy took the sacks there an hour ago," Alastair told her. "I had a feelin' ye might want to watch over Georgette again tonight, so I asked him if he would. He couldnae believe the story I told him, but I've nay doubt he'll be back to see that we're well. And we can walk by Greyfriars in the mornin', to give that goose to wee Bobby."

"Thank you." She smiled. "I don't know how I managed to be so fortunate, but I will never take a moment for granted."

"Nor me," he promised. "But now that ye ken my Christmas wish, ye really ought to tell me yers."

She shook her head. "Maybe one day."

"As ye prefer." He feigned disappointment and sat down on the ground, shuffling back into the makeshift lean-to.

She joined him, wedging herself against him as close as possible, and opened up the waxed paper parcel of festive goods. She also opened her beaded reticule, now a vessel for bread and butter, and set everything out on a blanket in front of them. A strange, yet perfect picnic.

"Do they ken ye took all this?" Alastair asked, wide-eyed.

Fiona nodded. "They insisted."

"I cannae remember the last time I had a Christmas dinner. Even cold, this is... wonderful," he said, hesitating. "Are ye sure ye want to share? Are ye nae hungry?"

"Eat as much as you please. I am as stuffed as that poor goose." She chuckled. "Just save me a mince pie. I want to eat them together, watching the city, saluting the end of Christmas until next year."

He took a piece of goose and put it on a bread roll. "Now that ye've agreed to marry me, ye realise ye'll have to help me make the toys, do ye nae?"

"You just try and stop me." She leaned into him, listening to the distant voices of a choir singing their evensong. There was no snow falling from the skies, but the blanket that covered the earth was still fresh and thick, twinkling like diamonds in the moonlight.

"Another good year, eh?" he said, chewing quietly.

She peered up at him. "The best, my love."

I wish that every year might be better than the last, she prayed silently, for though there were still a few hours until midnight, she did not want to risk waiting until the last moment to make her Christmas wish. Although, with Alastair at her side, his love for her radiating, she wondered if she had already been granted a wish that year.

Chapter Twenty-Two

New Year's Day arrived with a downpour of icy rain to slough away the slush of the last snowfall, and whilst others ran for cover from the deluge, seven figures huddled outside the main gates of the gaol, waiting impatiently beneath the grey skies.

Fiona held her breath as the gates squealed, creaking open just wide enough for a single person to squeeze through. And one person did, shoved by a rough hand. He stumbled forward, a shadow of his former self.

Thin and bedraggled, wearing a threadbare mockery of the clothes he had been wearing when he was arrested, Fiona's father seemed to have aged a decade in a year. His skin was as dull and grey as the sky overhead, his eyes sunken, his lips cracked, whilst sores blotched his body.

But the moment he saw his wife and daughter standing there, alongside Tommy and Alastair, Mrs. Ogilvy and the Arbroaths, a smile cracked his drawn face, and it was like the sun coming out from behind the rainclouds. Spring coming early.

"My love," Beryl whimpered, rushing forward to embrace her husband.

His thin arms encircled her, his eyes closing in something like relief as he held her to him, swaying the way they used to in the kitchen of their New Town apartments.

Fiona held herself back though she, too, longed to run to him. Her mother needed this, and considering Fiona had waited a year, another few minutes would not kill her.

George Arbroath had been true to his word, summoning the power and influence of his most prominent friends the day after Christmas.

Fiona suspected he had appreciated the distraction, throwing himself into the mission of freeing Donal McVey so as not to concentrate on the quietness of the townhouse and the presence that would forever be absent. After all, Harriet now had Beryl to distract her, but he had nothing.

On the afternoon of New Year's Eve, George had entered the townhouse like a whirlwind, crying out the good news that the sentence had been overturned and that Donal was to be released the following morning.

It had woken Fiona, who had been sleeping after a night at Georgette's grave, and he had promptly insisted that everyone enjoy an impromptu celebration.

They had supped good wine and eaten good food, and though spirits had been high, the little party had eventually turned into a memorial of sorts—a celebration of the short life that Georgette had lived. And though it had been sad, it had brought Fiona closer to the cousin she had never met; a rare gift that she appreciated.

As it turned out, Georgette's passing had not been entirely unexpected. She had been sickly since birth, yet defiant in her zeal for life.

But as she had grown older, it had become apparent that she would not outlive her parents, and though that had dampened her spirits for a while, she had been courageous to the very end, preparing her parents as best she could for the day that she would not be there anymore.

"I will send you miracles," she had, apparently, promised, just days before she succumbed to an affliction of the lungs and heart. *"I will send you signs that I am not gone, merely... elsewhere. So, you must promise me that you will not grieve, but that you will celebrate me, and remember me as someone who made the most of the time they were given."*

"And she did send us a miracle," Harriet had said, during that New Year's Eve party, having imbibed rather too much. *"She sent you both to us, and just as darling Fiona is to be wed! I would not have forgiven myself if I had missed her wedding."*

Fiona knew that her aunt would always see Georgette in her, but the flinching had lessened and the descent into inconsolable sobbing had ebbed, and if Harriet wished to see Georgette's life vicariously through Fiona's, then who was she to argue?

"Ye're too grown now to hug yer da?" Donal said, pulling Fiona out of her thoughts.

Grinning and tearful, Fiona ran to her parents, encircling them both in her arms as she held on tight. They held her back with equal fervour, all three of them sobbing and murmuring "I love you" as their fractured world knitted itself back together. Soon, her father would put on weight and have his health restored, and all his suffering through the past year would be a distant nightmare, long forgotten. At least, that was Fiona's dearest hope.

"Now, I recognise ye," her father said, lumbering toward Tommy to shake his hand. But Tommy grabbed him and hugged him instead, both men smiling with relief and gratitude. "And I mostly recognise ye," Donal added, chinning toward Alastair. "But I daenae ken the rest of ye. Apologies. Me mind isnae exactly what it was."

Beryl took her husband by the arm. "It is a long and curious story, but there will be time for all of that soon enough. For now, my sister has had a New Year's Day dinner prepared for you, and there is a soft, warm bed waiting, so you can sleep away the last year."

"Yer... sister?" Donal's eyebrows shot up.

Beryl smiled. "I told you, it's a long and curious story. Come, let's leave this place before they change their mind and try to drag you away from me again."

"Very well, but ye'll have to give me some bits of the tale on the way, else me head might burst," Donal replied, turning his head to kiss his wife.

Together, the eight figures made their way to the two waiting carriages, despite Donal trying to veer off to follow the path he might once have taken to his New Town apartments. Beryl had to steer him towards the carriages, explaining that, though they no longer had their home, they had the next best thing—they were together again, and they would find their feet once more, once he was safe and well.

"Are you coming?" Fiona asked, reaching the door to Mrs. Ogilvy's carriage.

Alastair pulled a face. "Am I allowed? Am I nae dressed too shabby?"

"You'll soon be part of the family," she told him. "You *must* come with us. After all, you played a rather large role in the events of the last year. It would be a pity to have to describe it all without you, and you really should, at some point, ask my father's permission to marry me."

Alastair frowned. "Yer permission isnae enough? Does this mean ye might nae be me wife?"

"Nothing can prevent it," Fiona answered, leaning down to kiss him from the carriage steps. "But my father would appreciate it, as I'm certain he would appreciate getting to know the man who oversaw the duties of Father Christmas in his absence."

Alastair blushed slightly. "Well, ye'll have to tell me what knives and forks to use."

"And glasses," she reminded him, pulling him into the carriage behind her.

A short while later, the carriages trundled away from the gloomy exterior of the gaol, wielding all of the people Fiona loved most in the world to the warm welcome of the Arbroath townhouse, where a festive feast awaited. It was not Christmas anymore, but perhaps there was still some Christmas magic in the air—a last sprinkle, bringing peace and joy to their corner of the world, as a new year began with the greatest gift of them all: hope.

Epilogue

Edinburgh, 1864

The toyshop spilled glowing light onto the pavement, the frost glittering.

Two enormous nutcrackers stood sentinel at either side of the shop entrance, delighting the children who raced inside to coo and squeal over the latest clockwork creations.

A Christmas tree twinkled in the corner, the small candles kept out of reach of the children thanks to a fence that encircled it, the slats painted to look like snow-covered branches.

Not a single speck of the shop had avoided the decorating talents of Beryl and Fiona; wreaths, bunting, velvet bows, holly leaves, and the most exquisite German tinsel that gleamed when it caught the light.

Outside the shop, next to the nutcrackers, a group of singers carolled through the favourites, whilst a barrow offered mulled cider and another barrow offered roasted chestnuts to anyone who came into the shop.

There was no place more festive, no shop more known for its merriment, and no toymaker more famous than the man who had given his name to the shop: *McVey's Toys and Wonderments*.

"Almost six o'clock," Fiona called from behind the counter, poking her head around the door that led into her father's secret workshop.

"Be out soon!" he called back.

Fiona smiled, feeling a little sorry for her father. With fame came responsibility, and at Christmas, everyone clamoured for his marvellous clockwork creations; not just in Scotland, but all across the British Isles. In the last three years, he had barely taken a single day of respite for himself, through sickness, through exhaustion, through everything, just so he would not disappoint any child.

And Fiona knew he had one last order to complete before he could close for Christmas Eve, for Christmas Day was one of the only days that he held sacred, spending it with his family.

"Is he finished yet?" Beryl wandered over from the pull-along toys that she had just finished dusting.

Fiona shook her head. "Soon."

"He said that an hour ago." Beryl could not help smiling, for no one could have been prouder of her husband.

Together, they had built something truly special. Of course, they had not done it alone, for Harriet had offered to give Beryl a hearty sum of money; her part of the inheritance she had been severed from.

For a while, Beryl had tried to refused, insisting she wanted nothing from the man who had cast her out, but after some discussion with Donal, and him admitting to his dream of a toyshop, the idea had come to her. Beryl had, at last, accepted the money and used it to buy the shop that had now become the centre of their world.

"He really is goin' to be out soon," Alastair's voice made Fiona turn, as her darling husband emerged from the secret workshop; his hands covered in paint, sawdust speckling his apron.

She smiled at him. "What *are* you two doing in there?"

"Makin' magic, my love." He swept her into his arms and kissed her, though there were still customers in the shop, trying to decide which toy would delight the most.

Fiona kissed him back, then quickly remembered herself and batted him playfully away. "You've been inhaling too many of those fumes," she told him, grinning. "You'll have us arrested for indecency."

"It would be worth it," Alastair replied, dusting off his hands. "I've left handprints on ye."

She took her mother's duster and brushed it against the marks, sweeping them off. "The gall of you."

"Would ye have me any other way?"

Fiona chuckled. "No, I wouldn't. Now, get back in there and tell my father to hurry. We have dinner to attend and then," she lowered her voice so the children would not hear, "presents to deliver."

"I'll tell him, but I cannae promise it'll help spur him on," Alastair said, retreating back into the workshop.

Ever since Donal's had recovered from his year in the gaol, Alastair had been apprenticing as a toymaker. One day, he hoped to take over the shop from Fiona's father, but until the day arrived when Donal was ready to retire, they were quite content to work together, making beautiful toys for those who could afford them and those who could not.

"You look happy," Beryl said, coming to lean on the counter.

Fiona nodded, settling her hand upon the slight rounding of her belly. "I am." She sighed contentedly. "I just keep thinking that, next year, everything is going to be so different. There's going to be a little person crawling around—the luckiest bairn in the world, having their pick of any toy they want. Still, it's… scary, in a way."

"You're going to be the best mother," Beryl assured. "I was scared too when I found out you were coming, but it is the greatest thing I have ever done. Being your mother."

"Being your daughter is the best thing I've ever done," Fiona replied, taking her mother's hand. "Has Aunt Harriet stopped purchasing things yet?"

Beryl snorted. "Not even slightly. You are going to have everything you could possibly ever need, and a hoard of things you likely won't, before this child comes into the world. She is excited, that is all."

"I'm grateful. I just wish she wouldn't spend so much on me."

Beryl shrugged. "Perhaps, you could give some of it to those in need. There will be plenty to share around."

"I might just do that," Fiona said, pondering.

In the near distance, the church chimed six o'clock, and the last few stragglers traipsed out of the shop, leaving Beryl and Fiona to do a final dusting and cleaning of the shelves and floors. Together, they dragged the huge nutcrackers inside and paid the barrow sellers for their wares and time, the carol singers wandering off into the night. That done, they turned the sign on the door to "closed" and waited for Donal and Alastair to appear.

"Is everyone gone?" Donal stuck his head out.

Beryl nodded. "No one here but us now."

"Is the carriage outside?" he asked in a hushed voice.

Fiona pointed to a fine carriage, decorated with festive bows. "I think that's ours, otherwise someone has been out there for a very long time."

"Quickly, then!" Donal urged, as he and Alastair began bringing out the sacks of toys that had been prepared for that night. A Christmas Eve tradition, worthy of repeating year after year.

Eking open the shop door, Fiona whistled, and Tommy came out of the carriage, darting across the street to where the sacks waited.

In something of a line, they passed the sacks from the shop to the carriage, glancing furtively up and down the street to make sure they were not seen by any children who might ask questions.

And when it was done, Tommy slammed the carriage door and climbed up onto the driver's bench with a proud grin upon his face.

"Daenae tell me wife, but this is me favourite night of the year," he announced, jamming a funny hat down onto his head: a curious pointed thing of dark green velvet, with a white bobble on the end.

Fiona laughed. "I think it's everyone's favourite night, but what *is* that thing on your head?"

"Ye daenae like it?" Tommy pouted. "Well, tough, 'cause it makes me feel jolly. Are we goin' to the cemetery first?"

Fiona nodded. "Christmas Eve dinner with Georgette, then straight out to our duties. I thought we could start with Nathan again."

The little boy that Fiona and Alastair had encountered three years ago had remained true to his promise of keeping the little drummer boy in perfect condition, and his spirits had improved with the years, always appreciating the clockwork gifts that came his way with wide-eyed enthusiasm.

Apparently, his father had finally left, but his mother seemed happier for it, allowing them a fragile peace.

"Are any of ye gettin' in? There's a wee bit of space for the lasses, I reckon," Tommy said, nodding down at the carriage door.

But Beryl put her arm around her daughter's shoulders, shaking her head. "I think we'll walk. It's a beautiful night and it would be a pity to waste it." She grinned. "You get to have my daughter, my husband, and my son-in-law all night, so I'm just gong to steal them for a short while."

"I'll see ye there, then," Tommy said, snapping the reins. The horses plodded off, pulling the carriage full of precious cargo.

Dragging on his coat, Donal blew out the last of the candles and lanterns and stepped out into the cold night, turning the key in the lock of the toyshop.

He slipped the key into his pocket and unleashed a happy, relieved sigh. "Now, me dears, the real work begins." He flashed a wink at Alastair. "I think this year might be the best yet."

"As do I," Fiona said, remember the wish she had made long ago. Thus far, it still seemed to be coming true.

Alastair came forward and took his wife's hand, leading the way to the cemetery.

Another tradition that was worthy of repeating, so that Georgette—the woman who had reunited a family from beyond the grave—would not feel like she was missing out.

They had taken to sharing a picnic there on Christmas Eve, no matter the weather, so no member of their family was ever forgotten.

"Are we takin' some goose for Bobby?" Alastair asked, already knowing the answer.

"A whole leg, if I can hide it without anyone seeing," Fiona replied, curving her body into her husband's, stealing his warmth as they made their way through the New Town.

An air of excitement pursued the quartet when they entered the cemetery, Donal beginning a round of "Deck the Halls" as they walked. It was impossible not to look forward to the night ahead, and even if everything changed with the arrival of Fiona and Alastair's firstborn, it was her fondest hope that the tradition begun by her father would continue for as long as people needed it, the mantle of Father Christmas passing from child to grandchild to great-grandchild, so that every worthy little soul could have a sliver of happiness each year, waiting for them with a ribbon tied around it. A gift that said, *you are important, you are worthy, and this is just for you.*

That would be the greatest Christmas wish of all, not requested from the heavens, but made together, on Earth. A wish that was already coming true.

THE END

I hope that you enjoyed this book.

If you are willing to leave a short and honest review for me on Amazon, it will be very much appreciated, as reviews help to get my books noticed.

Over the page you will find a preview of one of my other books

PREVIEW

The Blind Tailor's Daughter

Chapter One

York, Winter 1863

Drizzling rain hardened to ice on the shadowed cobbles of the city, as the bells of York Minster tolled the night warning to those who were not yet warm in their beds or safe behind closed doors and candlelight.

For the beggars and vagrants, refuge was sought wherever it could be found, those lost souls accompanied only by the mumble of their own voices, praying to be alive when morning came. Or not... for it was a hard life, made all the harder without family and friends to lean upon, and not two coins to rub together.

But above the sea-green exterior of Acklam & Sons, the amber glow that spilled out onto the ice-slicked street below could have flowed from the very hearts of the joyful family within, who were in the midst of a celebration.

"Six-and-ten is a noble age," Bonnie Acklam's mother, Clara, announced, as she produced something from behind her back. She set the gift upon the worn kitchen table, where the Acklam family of four shared all of their meals together, never wanting for much.

Bonnie gasped at the sight of the delicacy, her eyes as wide as the plate upon which the treat had been served. "This is too much, Mama! The neighbours will call us wasteful if they were to get a whiff of this!"

It was a cake, dripping white icing. A pound cake, all in honour of her sixteenth year upon this Earth.

"Don't you worry about the neighbours, lass. Let 'em be jealous. It's not so often that I get to spoil me eldest girl," her mother replied with a wink, her voice still carrying a hint of her humbler origins as a dairy maid in the wilds of North Yorkshire.

Bonnie's younger sister, Alice, licked her lips hungrily. At twelve years of age, nothing delighted Alice as much as the promise of sugar, for though the Acklam family were reasonably well-off, they were not frivolous.

They knew how fortunate they were when every winter brought frozen bodies in doorways, and the lines at the churches grew longer each year, when hot soup and bread was being offered to those in need.

As much as they could, the Acklam family shared their good fortune, making charitable donations and giving what they did not need to the poor, but it would never be enough to remedy the great plague of poverty that seemed to blight every city and town, and not just in Yorkshire.

"Might I have some?" Alice asked eagerly.

Clara chuckled and turned back to the stove to stir the thick, meaty stew that bubbled merrily. "When your pa comes up and you've eaten all your dinner—then, you can have some. Don't want you spoilin' your appetites."

"Shall I fetch him?" Bonnie said, rising from her seat. Her skirt and petticoats rustled as she moved toward the door, her ribs aching from the corset that she had only recently begun to wear. Yet, she tried not to complain, for the same reason she felt a touch guilty about the cake: she was lucky.

Clara did not look up from the pot on the stove. "Don't trouble him if you can help it, but see if he can't give you a notion of when he might be done. I don't want this stew thickenin' too much more, else it'll be like porridge."

"Yes, Mama." Bonnie swept out of the warm apartments and down a draughty stairwell, where the January wind whistled through hairline cracks in the wall.

She picked her skirts up as she went, terrified of tripping and falling down the steep staircase. Her friends liked to tell horrifying tales of such tragedies, scaring one another silly, for imagined calamities were the only things that they had to worry themselves about. In their warm residences, their bellies full, their hearts merry, their minds still innocent, they could take their time in growing up, safe in the knowledge that they would likely always lead a sheltered existence.

At the bottom of the stairwell, a long hallway led to the front door, where the rain peppered the wood like a shy passer-by hoping to gain entry. Another door on the left opened out into Acklam & Sons—Tailors and Dressmakers. An unusual combination of both arts in one shop, perfectly and famously articulated by Bonnie's beloved father: a gifted man and the son of the Acklam who had given the shop its name, though there were no more sons to carry it on. Clara had almost died giving birth to Alice and, since then, they had not been blessed with more children, but if Clara or her husband, Bernard, minded, they did not show it. Instead, they poured everything they possessed into nurturing their two daughters, ensuring they were educated, appreciative, and, most of all, kind.

"Papa?" Bonnie called out, as she swung open the door to the shop.

The shop had always appeared eerie to her, once it was devoid of customers and the lights were extinguished, leaving only the ghoulish shape of mannequins, dressed and ready for a ball. Bonnie could never shrug away the feeling that they moved of their own volition, creeping towards her as if they sought her flesh-and-blood existence for themselves.

She hurried through the gloom, illuminated only by the streetlamps beyond the leaded windows, until she reached the workshop at the rear.

The door stuttered for a moment as she tried to open it; the hinges swollen. Finally, with a reluctant wheeze, the door gave, sending her stumbling into her father's familiar domain.

Her father, hunched over his work in the farthest corner with his back to her, did not seem to notice the intrusion. His fingertips, pinching a needle, moved with the grace of a ballerina, looping the thread in and out of a cascading reem of red silk, the colour of garnet.

A bold choice of colour that Bonnie appreciated, wishing that, one day, she might be daring enough to wear such a gown to a ball or a gathering.

Of course, she would need to be invited to one first, but her father was never short on invitations to special occasions; he just never attended, seeing no reason to when his work spoke for itself. Indeed, after every illustrious soirée, whether it took place in York or London or Manchester or Bath, he found himself inundated with requests, each lady and gentleman vying for priority with as much money as they could reasonably muster.

But that was the mystery and appeal of her father's work: he accepted commissions only from those he chose to, refusing to buckle underneath the pressure of a thousand demands. The Acklam family could have been exceedingly wealthy, had he wanted them to be, but he was happy as long as his family had enough; he would not work himself to the bone for more than was necessary to be comfortable. Bonnie had always admired that about him.

Secretly pleased that her entrance had not been noticed, Bonnie lingered by the doorway, observing her father as he continued to work.

Other, finished masterpieces were hung upon mannequins or wrapped in pretty white boxes, tied with ribbons that were the same sea green as the shop's exterior, where they awaited collection from the errand boys and express riders who arrived each day.

The gentlemanly attire was pleasant to the eye, too, but Bonnie preferred to bask in the beauty of the intricate, exquisite gowns, revelling in the explosions of colour that brightened the otherwise plain workshop.

"Blast it all," her father muttered sharply, prompting Bonnie's heart to jump in her chest. He never spoke unkindly to her, never raised his voice to anyone, yet she had not mistaken the violence in his voice.

Bernard paused, setting down the needle and thread so he could bring the knuckles of his fingers to his eyes. He rubbed them, hissing in the back of his throat as if he was in pain.

A few moments later, he sat back on the worn, uncomfortable stool where he did all of his work—his wife and children had tried to insist upon a nice, wing-backed chair, but he had refused, explaining that "If I'm too at ease, I'll get nothing done." He stared up at the ceiling, narrowing and widening his eyes, blinking rapidly before resuming the vehement rubbing with his hooked knuckles.

"There's no time for this," he rasped at no one at all, for it appeared he still did not know he had company.

Returning his attention to his workbench, a horrified expression strained his still-handsome features, his fingertips fumbling across the dark green mats that caught stray fibres and severed filaments of thread. He closed one eye, huffing and puffing as he continued to skim his hands over the workbench, his demeanour growing more desperate with every passing second.

Has he lost his needle? Bonnie considered it to be the only explanation, and not so unusual; he was always losing needles and sending the girls out to purchase more from the haberdashery: a tiny shop, tucked away in the narrow lanes of the Shambles.

Bonnie loved being given the task, for walking through the Shambles made her feel as if she had been transported to a different century, her mind conjuring the sights and sounds of a bygone time when kings lopped off heads on a whim and feasted upon swans, holding medieval gatherings filled with smoke and mystery and gowns so ostentatious that the ladies could barely walk in them.

Bonnie's mother often told her that her daydreams were "ghoulish," but she preferred to think of it as being grateful for the current state of things—a country with an inspiring, venerable queen upon the throne who loved her husband and was dutiful to her subjects.

"The men will tell you otherwise, but women make for better monarchs," her mother had whispered to her one night. "They've a more sensible head on their shoulders. That's why there are men who'll look for any excuse to call 'em hysterical. Don't want us women gettin' ideas above our station."

The sentiment had stuck with Bonnie, giving her the—perhaps misguided—sense that she could achieve anything she set her mind to. What that might be, she was not yet sure, but she did know one thing: she would make something of herself, one day. She would be a woman to be celebrated, like Queen Victoria.

"Where is it?" her father hissed, drawing her out of the imagined streets of the Shambles and back into the gloomy workshop. His jaw clenched, a surprising curse of "Damn it all!" leaving his lips. Bonnie understood a second later, as he lifted his finger and put it in his mouth: he had found the needle.

Bonnie hurried to him. "Are you well, Papa? Did it prick you?"

Her father jolted as if she had leapt out of the shadows at him, his breath rasping from his lungs, his eyes wide in terror.

"It's me, Papa," she said quietly, panic bubbling through her veins as she noted his distress. She had not meant to scare him.

"I didn't know you were there," her father replied, after a moment; his breath slowing. "You gave me quite the fright. What have I told you about creeping up on poor souls?" He laughed, but it sounded forced, his eyes still wide to the whites.

"What's wrong, Papa?" Bonnie was no fool; she could feel the fear still emanating from him, his precious, gifted hands trembling. And she doubted it had anything to do with her sudden appearance.

He could not look her in the eyes. "I've got a gown that must be finished by the morning, and it's still in pieces. That's all, darling." He gestured to the door. "You go back upstairs and enjoy your birthday. Six-and-ten only happens once."

"All ages only happen once." Bonnie mustered a smile, trying not to let her worries get the better of her. If her father said it was just the stress of his work, it was her duty as his daughter to believe him.

Her father nodded, laughing faintly. "Quite right. I hear your mother made you a cake—have a slice and bring me one down in a while." He paused. "I'm sorry, but I'll have to stay in the workshop until this is done, though you must know I'd prefer to be up there, celebrating with my girls."

"I know, Papa." She put her arms around him.

He hugged her back with a ferocity that frightened her, for it was as if he was clinging to life itself, squeezing the air out of her lungs.

He must have realised he was holding her too tightly, as he slowly released her. "Go on now, and tell your mother I'm sorry, too. I hate to disappoint you all."

"You haven't disappointed us, Papa," Bonnie told him sadly. "We owe everything we have to you. I'll bring you the biggest slice of cake Mama will let me cut."

Her father flinched, confusing her. "Thank you, darling."

Pressing a kiss to his cheek, Bonnie turned and headed for the upstairs apartments, but as she reached the door that opened onto the interior hallway, she stopped and looked back. Her father must have mistaken the squeal of hinges for the door closing again, not realising she was still there, for as he sat upon his worn and rickety stool, he hunched over, holding his head in his hands, his shoulders shaking as if he were crying.

"What do I do?" he whispered to the gloom. "What in heaven's name am I to do?"

Bonnie slipped out as silently as she could, her heart thundering in her chest, tears pricking at her own eyes, for she knew her father; if something had brought him so low that he wept, it could not be anything good. Indeed, picturing the manner in which he had fumbled for his needle and rubbed his eyes as if he wanted to remove them from his skull entirely, she feared the very worst.

Chapter Two

At three o'clock in the morning, if the bells of York Minster were to be believed, Bonnie could no longer lie idly in her bed, worrying for the beloved father who had not yet surfaced from his suffocating lair. Crawling out from beneath the coverlets, listening to the soft, peaceful breathing of her sister in the next-door bed, Bonnie grabbed her dressing gown and threw it on as she slunk out of the bedchamber on tiptoes.

Passing through the kitchen, her gaze flitted toward the pot on the stove, and the half-circle on the table that had been wrapped in waxed paper: the remains of the stew and the cake, with plenty to spare.

Perhaps, he will have eaten something by now, she mused anxiously. Earlier in the evening, when she had taken a slice to her father, he had not taken so much as a bite. And when she had returned an hour later to collect the plate, it still had not been touched. Nor had the bowl of stew, which had congealed. As a man who abhorred being wasteful, the sight of that untouched bowl had terrified Bonnie far more than any curse word or strained insistence of all being well.

"Don't, darling," a soft, sad voice murmured, as Bonnie reached the door to the staircase.

Bonnie whirled around in alarm, spotting a shadow in the corner of the kitchen. She heard the scratch and hiss of a match being struck, carrying the stinging smell of sulphur to her nostrils. A moment later, a candle wick burst into life, illuminating the tired and pale face of Bonnie's mother.

"I thought I'd see if he'd eaten his cake yet," Bonnie said limply, her heart aching at the haunting vision of her mother, sitting in that darkened corner as if she was holding a vigil.

"He hasn't," her mother replied. "Just let him work, darling."

Bonnie frowned. "Is William with him?"

"No, he is alone."

"Should someone not fetch William?" Despite the hour, Bonnie was ready to fulfil the task, for if her father needed assistance, then it seemed only sensible that he should have his apprentice with him. It might even be a worthwhile education in how to complete a gown with time running out.

Her mother got up, the dancing shadows of the candle deepening the hollows around her eyes. "Your father doesn't want him sent for."

"Whyever not?" Bonnie's hand reached for the door handle.

Her mother sighed. "Because he has said so."

"And when have you ever done something because "Papa said so," if it was utter nonsense?" Fear held Bonnie's lungs in a winching vice, her throat tightening as her worries plumed, spreading into something monstrous that slithered through her body, tar-black and just as cloying.

"Just... let him be, Bonnie."

But Bonnie could not. She would not. "Very well, if no one will summon William, then I'll offer my services to Papa." She wrenched open the door. "I know enough to be of use."

As Bonnie headed down the stairs at a clip, her mother followed, moving as slowly as someone sentenced to death. A weight of resignation turned her mother's every footstep leaden, and like a mythical tale that Bonnie had read a while ago, the young woman did not dare to look back, fearful of what she might see. Yet, what lay ahead of her was, perhaps, even more frightening.

At the door to the workshop, Bonnie waited for a reprimand that did not come. Part of her wanted her mother to stop her, wanted an explanation, wanted to be assured that what she suspected about her father was nothing more than wild imagination, but there was only silence and the faint scream of hinges as she stepped into the workshop once more.

Her father sat where she had left him, sweat glistening upon his brow, perspiring under the heat of at least fifteen candles and lanterns that were arranged in a horseshoe around him. A bucket of sand occupied its own stool, within easy reach if sparks should fly and a fire should spread.

"Who goes there?" Bernard's eyes turned in his daughter's direction, and she prayed it was only the darkness beyond his ring of light that delayed his recognition of her.

"Bonnie wanted to see if you'd eaten your cake," Clara replied, resting a hand upon Bonnie's shoulder. "I told her to leave you be, but she insisted."

Bernard squinted, rubbing eyes that were already dappled with rough patches of red. Friction burns. "I didn't have much of an appetite, lass," he told his daughter with a smile so sad that it splintered Bonnie's heart. "But I'll have it for my breakfast."

On the workbench, piles of garnet silk were strewn in every direction, and Bernard's fingers were wrapped in thin bandages. For a man who relied upon a delicate touch for his craftsmanship, those bandages must have been a curse, making his needlework clumsy.

"What are you not saying?" Bonnie could hold her tongue no longer. "I am six-and-ten, not four-years-old. I am not a dolt. I know you are both hiding something from me, and… I would hear it from you instead of making my own guesses."

Her mother and father exchanged a look… or tried to. Her father squinted at the spot where he must have thought his wife was standing, but he was, in fact, staring at a supporting wooden pillar. Perhaps, Bonnie could have ignored that, but she could not ignore the pink hue, shot through with threads of livid red, that coloured the whites of his eyes. Nor could she neglect to see the crusts of dried-up secretions that clung to his lashes and gathered in the corners of those corrupted eyes.

"Are you unwell?" Bonnie pressed when she received no answer from her parents. "Shall I send for a doctor?"

Her father sighed and shook his head, setting down a scalloped sleeve that, even at a distance, appeared crooked.

"The doctor has been, several times. There's nothing he can do for me." His brow creased as he glanced down at his hands, bringing them up to his face until his palms were almost touching his cheeks. "I thought it would pass—the doctor said it might—but it has not. And you are quite right; I shouldn't hide this from you any longer, though I must urge you not to say anything to Alice."

"I won't breathe a word," Bonnie promised, wringing her hands.

"I am losing my sight, dearest Bonnie," her father began in a heavy voice. "This past week, it has been fading more quickly than before. I... thought I had longer, but... my sight is almost gone." His breath caught as he spoke, hitching every few words as if it was a terrible struggle to admit the truth. "I can see shapes, I can see light and shadow, I can see everything in a blur, but the details of things—it is impossible. I can't do... I can't..."

Even though she had seen her father weep, it was the first time she had seen him break. It was akin to watching a person collapse in on themselves, the essence of who they were crumbling to dust, leaving a husk behind. Her father did not even cry, this time; he simply stared blankly down at the cresting waves of red silk that he could not see properly, his body trembling as if the cold of outside had snuck in through the cracks in the windows and in his very soul.

Bonnie rallied, swallowing down her own despair as she went to her father. "What can I do? My stitching has vastly improved, and I've watched you enough times to be of help. Tell me, Papa, what do you need? I won't sleep until it's done, and after that... well, we don't need to think about that, right now. Let's concentrate on just this one gown."

"It's too much," her father replied, shaking his head. "It can't be done."

"It can and it will," Bonnie insisted, removing the sand bucket from the nearby stool and taking her place at her father's side. "So, instruct me."

Across the workshop, Bonnie's mother observed the scene with shining eyes. She sniffed and turned her face away, discretely brushing something from her cheek as she strove to steady her breaths.

How long have you known, Mama? Bonnie wondered. How long have you carried the burden of worry by yourself? She thought of the cake and her stomach sank, for that confection might have been more costly than she realised: a luxury that they could not afford, if her father could no longer work.

"The inlay needs to be sewn into place," her father began hesitantly, moving his stool along the bench so Bonnie could sit in front of the fabrics. "That black material, there. And when that is done, everything needs to be sewn together. The entire gown. I... I'm sorry, Bonnie."

Bonnie put on her best smile. "Don't apologise, Papa. Just teach me. Pretend I'm William." She hesitated. "Shouldn't we send for him? Two pairs of hands might work swifter than one."

"No," her father replied sternly. "William is not to know."

Read The Rest

Printed in Great Britain
by Amazon